MOUNTAIN STRUGGLE

BY THE SAME AUTHOR

Mont Blanc Rescue Series
Book 1: Mountain Struggle
Book 2: Mountain Impact

**

Sharp's Cove Series
Book 1: One Night Years Ago
Book 2: Two Favors Repaid
Book 3: Three Times Ablaze

**

Grim Reapers Series
Book 1: Storme's Match
Book 2: Sawyer's Mistake
Book 3: Prado's Choice

**

Standalone Novella
Cold and Bitter Snow

Mountain Struggle

Mont Blanc Rescue

Book 1

J.R. Pace

Mountain Struggle

Published by J.R. Pace

Copyright 2021 by J.R. Pace

Cover design by Maria Spada

ISBN: 978-84-09-33348-6

Note to readers: This book contains adult scenes and language, and is intended for adult readers.

The mountain is my domain.

-- Gaston Rébuffat

Chapter 1

Damien

Damien Gray stood up, stretching to relieve the kinks in his neck and shoulders. He wasn't sleeping well these days, and sitting at his desk most of the day hadn't helped.

He wondered if he should be upgrading his bed to a Super King—in recent months Jamie, his six-year-old son, had made a habit of wandering into Damien's bed sometime between three and four in the morning. The boy was typically fast asleep minutes later, but by then it was too late for Damien—he was fully awake.

He often spent an hour lying beside his son, watching his little chest rise and fall gently, before giving up and getting out of bed. Asleep, Jamie seemed younger than his six years, and Damien was often returned in his mind to the moment four years earlier when the boy's mother had turned up on Damien's doorstep with the toddler in tow.

Damien looked down at his watch—almost five p.m., and he still had to stop by the store on his way home. He and

Jamie were going to teach Tess, Jamie's nanny, how to cook chicken fajitas.

As always when he thought of Tess, he felt a completely inappropriate surge of desire course through him.

Stay away.

She's twenty-five years old, and she's great with Jamie.

Don't fuck it up.

Damien turned off his computer and lined up the papers on his desk. He'd have to come in early tomorrow to wrap up a couple of reports, but it was worth it to spend the evening with his son.

His hand was already on the door handle when his cell phone rang.

"Gray," he answered, forcing himself to tone down his impatience.

"*Commandant?*" The word was spoken in a lilting Canadian accent.

Damien and Drake Jacobs, his second-in-command at the Chamonix *Peloton de Gendarmerie de Haute Montagne*—PGHM for short—had worked together long enough that, as soon as he heard the other man's somber tone, Damien knew his dinner plans would have to be put on hold.

"We just got a call from Cosmiques. Two climbers went out on a climb early this morning, they were expecting them back for a late lunch, but they haven't arrived yet."

"Where are you now?"

"In the car, on my way to the office."

"Can you pick me up?"

"Sure thing, I'll be there in three minutes, *Commandant.*"

There was a time when getting ready would have involved little more for Damien than grabbing his uniform

8

jacket and the pack he kept ready, but that was before he had a son.

He sat down behind his desk again, feeling every one of his thirty-six years, and sighed softly before picking up the phone. It rang three times before anybody picked up on the other end.

"Hello?"

"Tess? It's Damien. Is Jamie there with you?"

She sounded slightly out of breath. "He's under the couch. I'm under the kitchen table. We're playing at being whales."

Damien smiled despite himself. His son's imagination never ceased to amaze him—it was definitely not something the boy had inherited from him.

"Should I put him on?" she continued in her soft Oxfordshire accent.

"No, please don't." He and Jamie didn't communicate well on the phone, perhaps because their only phone interactions happened whenever Damien was cancelling plans on his son—something that happened altogether too frequently. "Something came up … I'm not going to make it to dinner."

There was a moment of silence. Tess knew how much tonight's dinner meant to Jamie.

"I'm sorry," he continued. "I need to go up to the Aiguille du Midi station. I don't know what time I'll be home. Please tell Jamie—"

"It's okay, you don't have to explain," she interrupted quietly. Then, in a louder voice, "Jamie and I were thinking of visiting John. He might make us raclette for dinner."

"Raclette!" cried out a little voice. "Papaw's going to make raclette for us!"

"Yes! Let me call him and find out if he's home," Tess said. She was still holding the phone to her ear, but clearly wasn't speaking to Damien anymore.

Something swelled in Damien's chest. Tess had done it again—managed to distract Jamie so the boy wouldn't realize that Damien had let him down again. A part of him knew this wouldn't last—soon Jamie would be too old to be so easily tricked. But not today.

"Thank you," he breathed.

"We'll be here when you get back," she said. "Stay safe."

Damien's phone pinged with a message from Drake.

Be there in two minutes.

Damien put on his tactical jacket and changed into his boots, making sure the liners of his tactical pants were inside the boots. Even in the middle of summer it got cold up in the mountains.

He sent his father a quick message, letting him know Tess was going to call him. He wrote in English. Though Damien was born and had always lived in France, his American father had always spoken with him in English, and Damien was equally comfortable in both languages. It sometimes seemed to Damien that, forty years after moving to Chamonix, his father still spoke French like he'd only just arrived.

Though he and his father were very different and had grown apart since Damien's mother's death, Damien knew he could always count on his father where Jamie was concerned. Most importantly, should something happen to him, he knew John would take good care of Jamie. It was the reason he could do what he did, as a single father— otherwise, the risk would have been too great.

He pressed send on the message and put the phone back in his pocket, his attention now focused on the missing climbers.

#

The mountain hut's manager shrugged. "Normally we wouldn't even have noticed they were missing until nighttime, but Mr. Reeds was very particular about lunch being served for them at two p.m. in the upstairs terrace."

"Do you know why that is?" Damien asked. The Refuge des Cosmiques was incredibly popular with mountaineers and skiers, but wasn't known for providing special service to anyone.

The manager looked at him impatiently. "Yes, of course I know. He's going to ask *Mademoiselle* Lefevre to marry him as soon as they're back from their climb. He's planned a lovely proposal."

And no doubt given you a nice tip for your troubles.

"And you're sure they went to La Rébuffat?"

"Of course I'm sure," the manager huffed. "The two of them spoke of nothing else last night. The lady's climbed it several times before."

Damien looked down at his notes.

"So Mademoiselle Lefevre is a strong climber."

"Stronger than him, for sure. Poor Mr. Reeds was a wreck last night thinking about it. He said it was his first multi-pitch climb."

"And they went out alone?"

The manager nodded. "They left at four-thirty this morning."

A muscle ticked behind Drake's jaw, and Damien knew his friend was thinking the same thing he was.

Those two shouldn't have been anywhere near La Rébuffat — at least not on their own.

"Thank you for your help, *Monsieur* Lagarde."

"Jacques. Please call me Jacques. Let me know if we can help in any way."

Damien and Drake turned around and walked to the helicopter, where Lieutenant Kat Barreau, their pilot, waited for them. Beside her stood two lean, strong men, one of them dark-haired, the other one with hair so blond it was almost white.

"Gael," said Damien, addressing the tan, dark-haired man. "What are you doing here? I thought you were off today."

Gael turned and looked up at them. At five-eleven, he was a few inches shorter than Damien and Drake. His dark green eyes crinkled at the corners when he smiled, pointing towards the climbing packs on the ground next to them.

"This is what I do in my time off, *jefe*. Rémy and I were climbing nearby, so we came over to help." Gael León was their team's most experienced climber.

Damien nodded his head at Rémy, a mountain guide and avalanche forecaster from St. Gervais who often volunteered with the PGHM. Damien knew Gael and Rémy often went out to conquer impossible climbs together.

"How's my favorite NATO team doing?" Rémy asked, flashing very white teeth.

"Don't call us that," Gael asked, sighing dramatically.

Damien laughed. Rémy was referring to the multiple nationalities that made up Damien's team. Only he and Kat had been born in France, and in Damien's case he was only half French. The rest of the team had come to Chamonix from elsewhere. They all spoke at least decent French—you couldn't become a member of the PGHM without it—but each had excelled in other areas of their training.

Drake Jacobs, his Canadian second-in-command, was bilingual, of course. He was also one of the strongest men Damien had ever met—both physically and mentally. Hiro Habu, the son of a famous Japanese model and a French businessman who had come to France in his early teens, was the best dog handler Damien had ever encountered. Gael, a world-famous climber and tracker from Mexico City, had come to Chamonix for a summer of climbing and never left. Jens Melkopf, their team's doctor, had joined them after spending a decade with the German Special Forces. And of course, Kat Barreau was the kind of helicopter pilot who could land the helicopter on a coin, in the middle of a storm.

"It's good to see you too, Rémy. Glad you're both here," Damien said, sobering up. "I think we're going to need your help."

Drake summarized the situation for them. "The missing climbers, a man and a woman, went out early this morning to La Rébuffat. It was the man's first multi-pitch climb, and they haven't returned yet. It's six-thirty p.m. now, which means we have a couple hours of daylight left to find them."

"What are we waiting for, then?" Gael said. Damien understood the younger man's urgency—he felt it, also, although his job was to temper that urgency with caution. The truth was, mountain rescue was intense—the rush was similar to that of leading a hard pitch, except you also knew you were helping somebody in the most terrifying moment of their life.

"I already checked at the Aiguille du Midi station, and nobody matching their description took the cable car down this afternoon," Kat said. "Get in, we'll circle around La Rébuffat to look for them."

Somebody's flash went off in his face. Damien squinted and jumped up into the helicopter, glad to get away from the growing crowd. This was a common occurrence for them, as his team's appearance often caught the attention of visitors. The helicopter's presence, in particular, seemed to feed into people's morbid curiosity as they whispered among themselves, wondering what was going on.

The helicopter rose swiftly into the air. Outside the window, the mountains rose around them, tall and majestic. Damien couldn't imagine living anywhere else—that, along with his mother's illness, were the reasons he'd returned right after university.

Out here, in the mountains, one could walk for miles without bumping into another human being—and yet, never be alone. The dry smell of the rocks, the damp smell of the velvet trees in the summer and the frosty snow in winter, the voices of the people he'd climbed with in these mountains in the past—they were always with him up here.

A few minutes later, Kat spoke over the headsets they were wearing. "Look right, that's La Rébuffat." As well as being an excellent pilot, Kat knew the area like the palm of her hand.

"What is it, a 6a climb?" Damien asked.

Gael and Rémy both nodded. "It's a 6a, yes, but it's a long, technical climb."

"One of our two climbers has apparently never done a multi-pitch climb before," Drake said.

Gael shook his head. "And they chose La Rébuffat for their initiation? That's nine or ten pitches."

Damien said nothing. If they commented further, he'd have to remind his team it wasn't their job to judge people's actions, only to support them in making the right decisions and, where that was no longer possible, do their best to help them if they got in trouble. But nobody said anything else.

"Do we know how they're doing in terms of equipment?" Rémy asked.

"They left most of their things at the refuge. They were spending two more nights there, then going back home."

Kat interrupted them on the headset. "I see something, there, on the south face."

At first, Damien couldn't see anything. Kat's visual acuity had tested at 20/10, so that wasn't surprising. As they got closer, Damien saw it as well—two small, dark shapes huddled on a ledge.

Drake brought out a pair of binoculars. "That's them. A man and a woman. The man is signaling to us."

"They must be three pitches up."

Damien addressed Kat on the headset so everybody could hear. "Can you put the helo down in that clearing below, Kat?"

She nodded. "Of course. What are you going to do?"

"We'll climb up to them and figure out if we can move them. Be ready for take off, we might need to get them to the hospital."

"So who's climbing?" Gael said, rubbing his hands together.

"Is that you volunteering?"

"Always, *jefe*. You know that."

"I volunteer as well, *Commandant*," Rémy said. "We brought a lot of rope with us."

Damien nodded, looking at the two men. They'd both spent the day in the mountains, probably climbing hard, yet here they were, willing to climb again.

Drake didn't say anything. Each member of their team knew his or her strengths. Drake was a powerful athlete, but at two hundred and forty pounds climbing wasn't his forte.

"Gael and I will go up and evaluate the situation," Damien decided. "Drake and Rémy will wait below to help us on the way down."

Kat set the helicopter down smoothly. "Stay safe, guys," she said.

The four men got off, carrying all the equipment they were going to need. Estimating the distance between them and the rescues, Damien coiled the longest length of static line around his upper body. It'd be cumbersome during the climb but, if there was a chance to bring the couple down that way, they would need a long enough line.

They emptied their packs of anything that might not be essential but left their water bottles, clothing and first aid equipment. They didn't know what they would find when they reached the couple.

Gael, being the strongest climber, led the climb. Damien settled to belay him on the first pitch.

"I free soloed this just a few weeks ago," Gael said, his tone easy, as he started climbing. Damien knew the man was

16

a risk taker, but to hear him speaking so calmly about free soloing, where ropes weren't used at all and any mistake was, by definition, fatal, bothered him.

"Not interested. Keep clipping on to those bolts, Gael," Damien warned.

"Relax, *jefe*. I know what I'm doing, and we're working. I'm not going to take any risks with your life or theirs."

Damien noticed Gael didn't say anything about taking risks with his own life, but chose not to say anything.

Gael reached the top of the first pitch and secured himself to the wall. Damien waited for the thumbs up signal before starting to climb himself. His tight shoulder muscles complained, and he gritted his teeth. If the pain didn't subside, he was going to need to visit a physiotherapist at some point.

He reached Gael and kept climbing—it was his turn to lead in the second pitch. They'd done this so many times before, they didn't even need to speak. Once Damien had secured himself, Gael began climbing again. Damien couldn't help but admire the ease with which Gael moved, as if he were part of the rock he was ascending. Finally, Gael overtook him, leading in the third and final pitch.

After forty-five minutes of climbing, Damien reached the ledge where they'd seen the couple. He stood up and stretched his arms and legs gratefully. Unlike Gael, who wasn't even breaking a sweat, he felt every one of his thirty-six years.

Gael had already clipped himself to the wall, and Damien wasted no time doing the same. It was over three hundred feet to the ground—a fall from that distance was not something either of them wanted to consider.

The ledge was wider than it'd looked from the helicopter—enough that Damien imagined it'd be a magnificent spot for a picnic. Not that he or Gael were admiring the view right now.

Damien quickly approached Gael and the pair on the ground. He struggled to remember their names—Mr. Reeds and Miss Lefevre.

Gael was speaking calmly to the pair.

"My girlfriend is hurt," the man interrupted, shouting. "My phone doesn't work, we've been here for hours!"

Why do people come all the way out here and expect their phone to work as if they'd stayed in the city?

Swallowing his irritation, Damien kneeled beside the prostrate climber. Her lips were pulled at the corner, but her eyes were calm. He noticed with relief that she was clipped in to a bolt on the wall.

One less thing to worry about.

"We're here to help, Miss Lefevre. Can you tell us what happened?

"Aline," she said, shaking her head.

"Aline," Damien agreed easily.

"We were climbing, doing pretty good time—for us, I mean, we're not competitive climbers. I put my foot on a large foothold and suddenly felt my foot swing out from under me. I heard a distinct pop on the outside of my ankle … I haven't been able to put any weight on it since then."

Damien and Gael exchanged a quick look. Though both men kept their expressions neutral, they were both relieved.

She might not enjoy the trip down, but we can move her.

Time was of the essence now, however, as it'd be getting dark soon.

The man looked around nervously. "Is it just the two of you?" he asked, looking over the edge as if he expected a flying platform to appear and magically take them home.

"It's just us. Don't worry, Mr. Reeds, we know what we're doing," Damien said confidently. He focused on the woman again.

"Aline, I'm going to lift the leg of your pants and look at your ankle, okay?"

She nodded, clenching her jaw in preparation. As he'd expected, her ankle was swollen and extensively bruised. It was at least a Grade III sprain, but an X-Ray would be required to rule out an ankle fracture.

"Okay, good," he said reassuringly. He dug into his first aid kit. "There isn't much we can do up here to make you more comfortable, but I'm going to put an air splint around your ankle to immobilize it."

Aline didn't make a sound as he slid the splint on over her climbing shoe, but her nostrils flared visibly. She was in a lot of pain.

"Easy now, almost ready." He kept his tone nice and easy. Talking to a rescue was an art—you had to find the right tone to soothe and inspire trust, but not sound patronizing.

While holding her ankle still, he cautiously zipped the splint up, then lowered his head and started blowing air into the inflation tube. He ignored her sharp inhale—he hated causing her pain, but this would make the way down more bearable.

"Can you get us down?" Aline asked, her fingers gripping his arm.

"We're going to get you down," he confirmed.

Behind him, Gael spoke softly to the man, draping a spare jacket around his shoulders. Damien realized he'd been so focused on the woman he hadn't paid enough attention to the man, whose erratic behavior was indeed consistent with a mild case of hypothermia. He must have taken off his jacket and given it to his girlfriend at some point—God only knew how long he'd been sitting out here in just a T-shirt.

Damien nodded to Gael.

"Okay. We're going to hook this rope to your harness, and we're going to belay you down—one at a time. You don't have to do anything—we'll do all the work from here. Just relax and use your arms to push yourself away from the wall if you get too close."

"I can't … I don't think I can do this." The man's Adam's apple bobbed up and down.

"I know you can do it, Mr. Reeds. And the time to do it is now. It's seven-thirty. Soon it'll be too dark to attempt it, and none of us are equipped to spend the night up here."

As if on cue, the wind picked up. It got cold in the mountains as soon as the sun disappeared.

"Can't you bring a helicopter to pick us up?"

Damien shook his head patiently. "There's no place to land it, and no way to load you onto the helicopter safely. The helicopter is already waiting below to take you to the hospital."

"Trust us, Mr. Reeds," Gael said, looking up from the work he'd been doing preparing the ropes. "We've done this before."

"It'll be okay, honey," the woman said. Despite her pain, it was clear she understood her boyfriend was in a worse place in his head. "You go first."

Her words seemed to move her partner, and he shook his head immediately. "No. No. You're hurt. You go first. I'll be fine."

We don't have time for this.

"Let's get you settled here, Aline," Gael said, grabbing the coil of static line they'd brought and attaching it to her harness.

"Isn't that rope too thin to be a climbing rope?" the man asked.

"It's static line," Gael explained patiently. "It'll serve our purpose better here."

"Are you ready?"

Damien lifted his radio and spoke with Drake below. "We're going to belay them down, Drake. Be ready for them. Aline's coming down first. She's got a bad sprain on her left foot. We've immobilized it but she can't put any weight on it."

"Understood. Rémy and I will be ready for her."

Working together, Damien and Gael belayed first Aline and then her boyfriend. By the time he and Gael reached the bottom, it was dark, and Damien was wishing he'd worn an additional layer of clothing.

The couple were already settled in the helicopter, wrapped in Mylar blankets. They were holding hands and whispering in each other's ear—Damien thought of what the hut manager had said, and hoped this would become just a story for the couple to tell their children and grandchildren.

Or maybe they'll break up next week.

Either way, it didn't matter. What mattered to him was that they'd both have the ability to make that choice. That was the single biggest reason he and his team did what they did.

Damien looked down at his watch. His son would probably be getting ready for bed already.

Chapter 2

Tess

Tess Porter leaned her head back against the comfy navy couch. The couch was 100% masculine, like the rest of Damien's house. Or rather, 100% masculine with toys strewn all over the place.

Something clenched in her lower belly, as it did every time she thought of Damien and his son—she loved Jamie, and loved the close relationship that existed between him and his father. She just wished she could see Damien as simply a father—as her boss—and stop thinking about him as a man.

She put the book down on her lap. It had nothing to do with the book, which was a romantic thriller by one of her favorite authors, but it was getting close to eleven p.m., and she was tired.

She knew she wouldn't be getting any sleep until Damien came home. She couldn't help but worry about him. He hadn't said much when he'd called earlier, but she knew the only reason he would have been heading up to the mountains in the evening was if somebody needed rescuing.

Damien led the Chamonix specialized rescue unit, the *Peloton de Gendarmerie de Haute Montagne*—not that she'd ever be able to say that out loud in her rusty French. That was one reason she'd come out to Chamonix in the first place, to improve her French. The second, and most important reason was, she needed time and a change of scenery to finish her novel — that was her biggest goal for the year, and she wasn't contemplating failure.

Finding a job as a live-in nanny had seemed sensible at the time — she'd get the experience of living in another country, and the time to write, and not have to worry about living expenses. She'd interviewed with four other families before settling on the Grays.

Damien had hired Tess as a nanny for two reasons: one, his hours were unpredictable, so he needed someone who could take care of Jamie when he was gone, but also, Damien wanted Jamie to grow up bilingual in English and French, like himself.

Not that I sound American.

She smiled to herself, thinking about the first video interview she'd had with Damien. He'd been looking for an American nanny. She was good at reading people and was certain he'd been about to dismiss her profile based on her British accent alone, until she'd made Jamie laugh with something she said. She'd been hired on the spot.

Or maybe not on the spot, as it'd taken her two months to make the move from Edinburgh, where she'd been wrapping up her master's degree in Creative Writing.

It'd taken that long to convince her family that she really wanted to do this, and that it was the right thing for her. Tess came from a close-knit family, and it hadn't been easy for them to understand why she would move to a small town in France to live with a stranger and his child.

Of course, she hadn't technically moved into Damien's house. She was here now, while he was working and Jamie was asleep, but she had her own studio in the backyard. It was the kind of room that made her think of one of her favorite authors, Virginia Woolf. Her studio, for she'd made it hers shortly after moving in, had become her place to think and write, the place where she prioritized that which she'd always wanted to do but had never dedicated enough time to.

As a boss, Damien was fair. When he asked her to stay late, he always made up for it later, giving her more free time to write. It was an arrangement that worked for both of them. The fact that she'd fallen in love with Jamie, to the point where caring for the boy no longer seemed like a job to her, was incidental, and not something she was planning on sharing with Damien.

A noise at the door had her getting up from the couch. As always when she saw Damien, she was struck speechless—with his dark hair, piercing blue eyes and strong features, he looked more like a movie star than a search and rescue specialist. Add in the fact that he was six three and looked like he could easily bench press her body weight, and it was no wonder she often felt like drooling.

Not appropriate.

He's Jamie's father.

Stop embarrassing yourself.

She sobered up when she saw him frown. He looked exhausted, like he'd just been pulled through an emotional wringer—which was probably the way his job felt every other day.

"Hi," he said. "I'm sorry I'm so late."

"Is everything okay?" she asked, feeling the inadequacy of her words. "Was everyone okay?"

His lips curved up softly, the smile transforming his expression.

"We found the two missing climbers, and they're going to be fine. So yes, everything's fine."

He was staring at her bare feet with an intensity that made her wish she'd worn her socks. She looked down at her toenails.

Perhaps he doesn't favor burgundy.

"Uh … Jamie and I had raclette for dinner with your father, then I read him a book before he fell asleep."

"That kid would eat raclette every day of the week if we let him. That was some good thinking on your part, Tess. Thank you. We'll make *fajitas* tomorrow."

Tess didn't mean to judge—she knew the man in front of her only missed doing something with his son when he absolutely had to—but she also didn't want Jamie to be disappointed again.

"Sounds great. I'll do the shopping in the morning, while Jamie's at school, and it'll be a surprise for him in the evening when you get home."

Damien gave her a sad smile. He was too smart not to realize what she was saying.

"I'm sorry I miss so many things. And I'm sorry you're having to take up the slack. Maybe you should take a holiday—go somewhere fun. Wherever people your age go nowadays."

People my age.

Ouch.

Damien was always talking about people her age, as if they were a whole other species, even though she knew there were only ten years between them.

Ten years is not exactly a generation.

"Stop with the guilt trip, Damien. It's fine. You're here now, and Jamie is fine. We had fun together, with your father. Have you had anything to eat? There are some leftover vegetables from lunch."

"No. Thank you, Tess. I'm going to go to bed."

She liked the intense way he stared directly into her eyes as he spoke with her. For a moment, Tess thought he might be about to say something else—then he closed his mouth and the moment passed. His arm muscles flexed as he took off his jacket.

"Yeah, me too."

Maybe a cold shower first.

She picked up her book and her cardigan, and left him standing in the middle of his living room.

Chapter 3

Damien

Damien had woken up that morning with his hand down his shorts. It was the sort of thing that used to happen to him in his teens, but not the way he expected to wake up at age thirty-six.

Thankfully, Jamie slept in his own bed all night.

He'd been dreaming of a green, lush garden. It didn't take Freud to explain that dream to him. He couldn't stop thinking about Tess. He wondered what she slept in—did she sleep in shorts and a T-shirt? Naked? He could picture her stretched out naked on the Queen-sized bed, all pale and pink except for those burgundy toenails.

He shook his head to clear an image that had no right to be in his head.

He almost hadn't hired Tess. In that first interview together, when she'd connected the camera, he'd been rendered inarticulate by her fresh beauty. She had green eyes the color of a mountain lake in summer, fine porcelain skin and a mouth that begged to be kissed. He'd wanted to reach into the camera to see if her dark blond hair was as soft as it looked.

He'd been about to end the call, knowing he couldn't hire someone so beautiful to care for his son, when she'd said something in a funny voice that had made Jamie laugh out loud.

None of the other candidates they'd interviewed, and he and Jamie had taken the job very seriously and had met over a dozen men and women together over a period of two days, had managed anything of the sort. His son was doing well, but he hadn't seen his mother since she'd left him with Damien when the boy was two years old, and Damien knew he might still be dealing with some abandonment issues.

So Damien had hired Tess, hoping she was simply one of those photogenic people who always looked great on camera—telling himself she was bound to be less attractive in person.

Except she wasn't, because the camera didn't do justice to her sunny personality.

She was one of those rare people who brightened every room she walked into. His father, never one to hold his tongue, had told Damien he didn't understand how someone like Tess could stand living with someone as sour as Damien.

Not that Damien thought of himself as sour. He was serious, yes—and busy—devoted to his job and to his child. There wasn't room for much else in his life at the moment, but he enjoyed the little things in life as well.

Now, four months later, he had to admit hiring Tess had been an excellent decision. In that time Damien had seen the relationship between her and his son bloom. Jamie adored Tess, and she was good for his son—the female role model his son had been missing.

If Damien had to suffer because of it, and live with a constant hard-on, then so be it. He was a grown man—he could deal with it.

He just needed to keep reminding himself that she was too young and completely out of his league—as he'd been doing all day.

"Is everything okay, boss?" Drake asked laconically, drawing Damien back to the busy office.

Damien realized he had heard none of what Drake had been saying the last couple of minutes. The whole day, he'd been distracted—he needed to get his head back in the game.

"Everything's fine, Drake, but I need to get home for dinner. I promised Jamie we'd make fajitas tonight."

Drake nodded. His friend didn't have any kids, but he was an unofficial uncle to Jamie, and understood Damien's need to be the best father he could.

"I'll finish the report and email it to you. You can read it tomorrow."

"I'll take a look when Jamie's asleep. Thanks, Drake."

Damien left the office in a good mood. He drove past the church and took a right, heading out of town—although he and his team made a good living, none of them could afford anything bigger than a studio on their salary, not in central Chamonix. It was the price they paid for living in one of the most coveted ski resorts in the world.

In fact, even though his place was on the outskirts of town—a single-family house with a lovely backyard—it was still not the kind of place he could have afforded. His parents had bought the land fifty years earlier, when Chamonix was still cementing its position as a premier skiing destination, and built the house over the next few years. It was the house

Damien had grown up in, and he loved every single square inch.

Three years earlier, when Jamie had arrived in their lives, and Damien had been looking to sell his one-bedroom apartment and move to a bigger place, his father had suggested they exchange homes. They'd met up at the notary to formalize the donation they each made for the other. It'd galled Damien, having to accept a gift that large, but his father had shrugged it away in that stoic way of his, never wanting to speak about it again.

As he drove, Damien started whistling—he was looking forward to spending the evening cooking with his son.

He half-expected Tess and Jamie to greet him from the kitchen as he walked into the house—Jamie was still at that age where he would drop whatever he was doing and run to give Damien a hug when he came home—but the inside of the house was dark.

Damien looked at his watch—six p.m. He looked at his text messages. Tess and Jamie had been doing all kinds of things together, since Jamie was still enjoying his summer holidays, and she never failed to email him in the morning to share their plans for the day with him.

He checked his email. They'd been heading out to Le Lavancher after lunch. Damien smiled. He knew exactly why Jamie loved that place so much, and it had nothing to do with the view—it was all about the homemade cakes he always convinced Tess to buy for him.

Still, they should have been home long before now. He checked the fridge and saw red, green and yellow peppers, chicken, *crème fraiche*—everything they'd need to make fajitas. He checked his phone again—there were no new messages from Tess.

He ran a hand through his hair, absently noting he needed a haircut.

A sinking feeling grew in the pit of his stomach. It wasn't like Tess to be late or, if she was, not to send him a message. Damien had to remind himself to breathe.

He knew he should take out the food from the fridge and start cooking. Tess and Jamie would be back any minute— Jamie would be hungry, and Damien would laugh about his minor panic attack.

But even as he thought all of this, he was putting on his dark and light blue uniform jacket again and heading back outside. Before he could convince himself not to, he dialed Drake's number.

"Damien? I thought you'd be elbow deep in salsa and guacamole by now," his friend said. It sounded like he was out on the street already.

"I need your help, Drake."

The other man must have heard something in his tone, because his footsteps ceased. Damien knew he had his full attention now. "Anything."

"Tess and Jamie aren't home. She told me they were heading out to Le Lavancher. They'll probably be home any minute but—"

Damien stopped and swallowed. He recognized the sour, metallic taste in his mouth— it was fear.

Drake didn't let him finish the sentence. "I'm stepping back into the office. Let me make a couple calls. Do you know how they planned to get there?"

Damien looked out towards the covered parking spot where Tess parked the small dark green Citroën she normally drove.

"I don't know. The car's not here. I assume she drove, at least as far as Les Tines. Maybe they took the train up the mountain afterwards."

"I'll call Les Tines and meet you outside the office. Pick me up in ten minutes."

"I'm sure you have other—"

"I really don't, Damien," Drake replied in a dry, no-nonsense tone. "Pick me up in ten minutes."

#

Four hours later, the heaviness in Damien's chest had settled into an agonizing weight.

They'd found Tess's car in the Les Tines station, as expected. The train conductor remembered seeing Tess and Jamie take the train up to the small hamlet of Le Lavancher. Tess had a return ticket as well, which hadn't been used.

They'd made it to the bakery—Damien knew that would have been one of their first stops if Jamie had anything to say about it—where the owner remembered the pair. According to her, they'd been talking of heading up one of the hiking paths to have their snack. She didn't remember which way they'd gone—it'd been a glorious summer afternoon, and there'd been lots of other families and children looking to buy cakes.

From that moment on, nobody had seen them again—it was as if the earth had swallowed them.

Damien's heart clenched at the thought that he might never find them. This was his son—and Tess was … this wasn't the time to examine what Tess was to him. He just knew he needed to find them. Tess would never have stayed out voluntarily. Something bad had happened to them.

Nobody needed to tell him, at eleven p.m., that it was time to call a stop to the search for the night.

They'd searched all around the village and found no sign of either Tess or Jamie. They needed to head up into the mountains now, but Damien knew better than anyone else that searching at night would be foolish—dangerous for the rescuers and not likely to meet with any success.

"We'll be back at first light, Damien," Drake said softly. His hand was poised on a map of the area. He'd already identified the three more likely paths they could have taken. Damien was glad for his friend's leadership—he himself had led hundreds of rescues in these mountains, but right now he didn't feel he could find his way out of a shoe box.

Beau Fontaine, commander of their sibling Annecy unit, called him on the phone.

"How are you holding up, Damien?" he said. The man's usually gruff voice was tempered with caution.

"How do you think?" Damien replied, then immediately wished he could take the words back. Neither Beau nor anyone from his team deserved his anger. "I'm sorry. That was uncalled for. I'm just—"

"I understand," Beau replied. "I just wanted to let you know my team will be ready at first light. We'll coordinate with Drake."

"Thank you. I appreciate it."

Damien hung up the phone and looked at his battery—
18% left. If nothing else, he'd need to find himself a charger.
He thought of the torch in the trunk of his car.

*If Drake drives back with somebody else, I can search on my
own, just for a few minutes.*

"Thank you all. I'll see you tomorrow," he told his team.
They'd all driven up as soon as they'd heard Jamie was
missing. Gael and Kat had driven up from the office right
behind him and Drake.

Jens Melkopf, the team's doctor, had come up shortly
after. Nobody wanted to say this out loud, but in a case like
this they all knew Jens was the most important person there.
The rest of them all had emergency medical training, but Jens
had spent ten years as a doctor in the military before joining
search and rescue, and he'd seen things the others could only
imagine.

Only Hiro was missing. He and Bailey, a black Dutch
shepherd, had been at a dog and handler event in
Switzerland and were driving back that evening.

"That's not going to happen," Drake said, reading his
mind.

"You're not staying here, Damien." He ran a hand
through his short brown hair. "We know better than to tell
you to sleep—hell, none of us will be getting any sleep
tonight—but we're not going to let you stay here and
endanger your life. We'll drop you off at home. You'll rest as
best you can—then we'll pick you up at first light to start the
search."

It was a long speech by Drake's standards. Damien knew
his friend was right, but still, the thought that his son might
be lost in the mountains, was tearing him apart. As

36

unreasonable as it might seem, he wanted to stay close to where his son had disappeared.

Damien hadn't been there when his son was born. He hadn't known of his son's existence, in fact, until his mother, a woman he'd dated briefly two-and-a-half years earlier, had shown up on his doorstep with the child in tow.

One look at the toddler was all it had taken for Damien to fall completely, irrevocably in love. During the visit, when Jamie's mother had expressed concern about her ability to provide a stable home for the boy during her travels, Damien had found himself offering to keep the child. The moment she'd said yes, he'd known it was the right thing, and he'd never stopped feeling grateful that she'd come to him.

"He was wearing a light jacket," Damien said, his throat tight. "Not nearly warm enough to spend the night out here."

"What color?"

"Red and blue."

"Good. That's good. We're going to find them, Damien," Drake said tersely. "Tess will take care of him in the meantime. You trust her, don't you?"

"I do," Damien said immediately. He realized there was no doubt in his mind that Tess would protect his child — if she was able to do so.

But what if something's happened to her? What if —

I have to find them.

Damien made a strangled sound. He'd go crazy if he kept thinking this way.

"Come on," Drake said, opening the passenger door to Damien's car. "I'll drive you home."

Damien nodded. He was in no shape to drive himself anywhere.

Chapter 4

Tess

Tess ran as if the devil were behind her—which he was, in every sense of the word.

It's not like she'd never seen a gun before. When she was little, her grandfather lived out in the country, and kept a rifle in his house for wolves. Damien also carried a gun—he'd showed her the safe he kept it in when he was home, to make sure Jamie never played in that area.

But she'd never, until today, had a gun pointed at her face—or, something she'd found even scarier, pointed at Jamie.

She tightened her hold on Jamie's wrist. The boy was fast for a six-year-old, but he was tiring, and she was almost dragging him behind her at this point.

She'd tried to make it sound like a game—we're going to run as fast as we can as quietly as we can—but Jamie was too smart to fall for it. He'd looked at her with those ethereally blue eyes of his, so similar to his dad's, and spoken softly. "I can be quiet, Tess. Don't worry."

Then he'd started running, as fast as his little legs could carry him.

But now he was tiring—hell, after six months in Chamonix she was in the best shape she'd ever been in her entire life, and she too felt like her heart was going to burst.

She slowed down marginally to look behind them. There was nobody there.

Have we lost him?

Is he even alone?

Her head shifted from side to side so fast she almost gave herself whiplash.

Yesterday, the man had come up to them shortly after she and Jamie had reached the waterfall. They'd only just sat down to enjoy the homemade cake they'd bought in the bakery. Afterwards, they were going to pick up some leaves and rocks for a project she wanted to do next week. Then they were going to head back down into town.

The man had been dressed completely in black, his face almost hidden behind a cap, dark sunglasses, and a thick brown and gray beard. Tess realized she still did not know what he looked like underneath under that paraphernalia.

He'd said good afternoon and asked her for the time— very politely. She realized now he was probably waiting to make sure there was nobody else around.

She cursed herself now, but her spidey sense hadn't been triggered at all. One moment she'd been looking at her phone to tell him the time, the next moment he'd lunged for her, grabbed her phone, and thrown it over the edge and into the waterfall below. Even then, it'd taken a moment for her brain to catch up with what was happening.

A dark, shiny gun had appeared in the man's hand. He'd forced them to take off their backpacks—hers containing their water and snacks and Jamie's containing a few toys, and tossed them over the edge as well. He'd then signaled for her and Jamie to walk ahead of him, further into the mountains. None of her questioning, pleading or cajoling had served any purpose.

At one point, Tess had noticed a bright spot of color on the ground. She knew exactly what it was—she'd stubbed her feet on them often enough at home—and looked at Jamie. The boy's hand was in his pocket. He had a few Lego bits in his pocket and was dropping them, like breadcrumbs.

Clever kid.

She looked behind to make sure their kidnapper hadn't noticed. She couldn't see exactly where the man was looking because of his dark sunglasses, but his expression didn't change, so she took that as a win.

When Jamie had started crying from exhaustion, the man had waved the gun in the direction of the boy's kneecaps. Tess had quickly stepped in to lift him onto her back piggy-back style. She didn't know what was going on but wasn't about to give him any excuse to hurt Jamie.

Finally, when she didn't think she could go one step further, they'd arrived at a ramshackle hut, half-hidden behind some trees.

The man had motioned them inside with his gun. He hadn't said a single word since he'd asked her what time it was.

Tess was so out of her depth, she had no idea what to do. The man was big and bulky, plus he had a gun. She had Jamie to think about. But she couldn't walk inside that hut. Who knew what was waiting behind the door—inside, he could do anything to them.

"No," she said, shivering in the cool evening air. "No."

The man spoke in English to her then, his voice cold and toneless now, so different from the friendly stranger who'd asked her the time just hours earlier.

"Walk inside or I'll shoot the boy, then tie you close to the window so you can watch what the wolves do to his body tonight."

She'd felt Jamie sweet breath in the back of her neck. His little arms had tightened further around her and she knew he was crying silently against her jacket.

"Don't hurt him," she said. "I'll do anything you want. Just don't hurt him. Please."

But the man had wanted nothing from her. She'd gotten a glimpse of a rustic living room area before they'd been shoved into a bedroom. The man tied her hands in front of her then left them there, locking the door behind them.

"I'm right outside," he said. "Don't try anything."

"What's this about? Please!"

"You'll find out, eventually. Now lie down and get some sleep. Don't give me a reason to come back here tonight."

Tess was grateful there was a full moon outside the window. She knew otherwise they'd be sitting here in complete darkness, as there was no electricity in the cabin.

Tess was amazed at Jamie's resilience. They'd both gone to the bathroom, and she'd made a cup with her hands so Jamie could drink from the tap, grateful that at least they wouldn't be dying of thirst. She'd happened to have a handful of almonds in her jacket pocket, so she'd given those to the boy, who'd taken them quietly and uncomplaining.

She'd found an old, tattered blanket in a corner and wrapped it around her and Jamie.

"It's going to be okay," she told him. "I'm not going to let him hurt you."

"My dad will find us," Jamie had said, then proceeded to fall asleep, his little body curled against hers.

She'd sat there, her back to the wall, listening to Jamie's soft breathing, as the temperature in the cabin got colder and colder. She pressed Jamie's small body against hers in an attempt to keep him warm.

Once in a while, she heard the man pace in the living areas outside. He wasn't sleeping either.

At four a.m. she'd heard the door slam. After that, there was complete silence in the cabin. Leaving Jamie asleep on the ground, covered by the blanket, she'd tiptoed to the door and listened for the longest time.

He's gone.

He's not here.

It wasn't just that the noises from the other room had stopped. It was a sense of emptiness where earlier she'd felt the threat. Tess didn't consider herself to be a very spiritual person, but something, some kind of instinct, told her it was time to run.

Get out of here now.

She looked out the window. It'd be easy for Jamie to get out—a bit of a squeeze for her, probably, but she could do it if she had to.

Now that she'd made up her mind, she didn't want to wait another second. Who knew where the man had gone, and how long it would take him to get back. Neither she nor Jamie had been hurt so far, but that could change anytime. She thought of the man's toneless, dead voice.

There was nothing in the room that would help her break the window, but she still had her house keys in her pocket. Tess took off her jacket, shivering in the cold night air, then grabbed the biggest key, the one that opened her little studio—she would not spare a thought for her cozy space and warm bed—and held it sharp-side out before wrapping the jacket around her hand and arm as tightly as possible.

Will this work?

You have to believe it will work.

Jamie is depending on you to figure a way out.

It was that final thought that gave her the courage to punch the glass with her covered hand.

She positioned the key so that it struck the glass first, but the force of the blow caused it to slip and it was her knuckles that ended up slamming against the glass. Jacket or no jacket, the pain was blinding.

Do it again.

Quickly, don't take the time to think about it.

She repositioned the key between her knuckles and punched, from a closer distance this time, aiming for the same spot. A spiderweb crack appeared on the glass, so small at first she thought she might be imagining it—but no, there it was.

Tess punched again, ignoring the bruising around her knuckles. Something told her this was their chance. The man had implied he had a plan for them, and his voice had been venomous as he did so. Tess didn't intend for her or Jamie to stick around to find out what it was.

Tears sprang to her eyes as she punched the glass again, but the spider crack grew quickly now. Finally, the glass shattered. She grabbed the remaining shards and broke them off, pushing them outside the window, making sure at least the bottom edge was clear of glass.

She unwrapped the jacket from around her hand. The knuckles were swollen and painful but there wasn't any blood—that was good, she didn't want to be running around the mountain with an infected wound. Her windbreaker was ruined, but she still put it on again after making sure the glass was all on the ground.

Next, feeling a bit like MacGyver, she folded the tattered blue blanket and placed it over the windowsill.

She breathed in and out twice to calm herself before waking Jamie with a hug and a kiss, inhaling that soft baby smell that she associated with him and him alone.

"Good morning Jamie, time to wake up," she whispered softly in his ear.

"Daddy?" he asked in a broken voice.

"It's Tess. We're okay, we're going to go find your dad now."

The boy's eyes opened and latched onto her face. She saw the moment he remembered everything that had happened. His little face scrunched up, but he didn't make a sound.

She grabbed his hand and helped him stand.

"We're going to be okay, Jamie. We just need to walk a bit now and find your daddy. I know he's looking for us," she said briskly.

This last bit was true. Damien would have realized something had happened when they didn't come home for dinner, and would have kicked off a search for them already. She knew him well enough to know he would leave no stone unturned in his search for his son—but the mountains were dangerous, and the rescue team might not be looking in the right place.

Wishing she'd told Damien exactly where they were heading, she tightened her hand around the boy's smaller hand.

"You okay, Jamie?"

She needed the boy alert and on her side, so she waited patiently until Jamie nodded.

And so they'd gone out the window and started down the mountain, carefully at first because it was still completely dark and she didn't want to stumble. A twisted ankle here could mean game over.

Tess couldn't for the life of her remember the path they'd taken the day before. She'd let fear take over and hadn't been paying enough attention.

Then she'd heard the front door slam and knew the man was back. All thoughts of caution left her mind. She tightened her hold on Jamie's hand and ran hard, hoping she was retracing their steps and not taking them in a completely different direction.

But now they'd been running for what felt like hours, and both she and Jamie were reaching the limits of their endurance.

Jamie tripped and almost took Tess down with him.

We need to find a place to stop.

Tess sat down and leaned back against a tree, clasping the boy to her. She stroked his cheek gently, only then realizing Jamie had lost his glasses somewhere along the way. Jamie had strong hypermetropia—without his glasses, he wouldn't have been able to see the terrain they'd been running on, yet he hadn't complained once. Tess was once again amazed at his bravery.

Just a few minutes and we'll start running again.

Chapter 5

Damien

Damien and Drake hadn't exchanged any pleasantries when Drake picked him up outside his house at four in the morning. Both men were dressed in tactical gear—their uniform almost fully navy blue except for the jacket which had a wide lighter blue stripe running along the chest and one shoulder.

In his hands, Damien cradled the cup of coffee Drake had brought for him. Drake had dosed it liberally with milk and sugar—the exact opposite of the way Damien usually took his coffee, but Damien knew he'd need the energy for the day ahead. Not that he could get much past the lump in his throat.

Between his feet sat a paper bag containing Jamie's pajamas, his favorite stuffed animal—a green pig called Tom—and one of Tess's sweatshirts.

Damien had spent half the night in Jamie's room, sitting on the boy's colorful racing car bed, barely able to breathe through the pain of not having him there. He was used to coming into his son's room and kissing his forehead when he came home, regardless of how late it was. Last night, all he'd been able to do was wonder where his son was, and if he was okay.

Damien had never felt so alone. He'd been tempted to call his father, but hadn't wanted to bother him on his once-a-year poker retreat. If they didn't find Jamie tomorrow, he'd have to have the world's most difficult conversation with the old man.

Afterwards, he'd walked out into the yard towards the small studio where Tess slept. He'd purposefully walked outside barefoot and in his shorts, shivering in the cool night air. It'd be even colder up in the mountains where Tess and Jamie were.

Is it too cold to survive the night?

Damien had spent the night outside with no shelter and little equipment, but he was a grown man and a survival expert. Tess and Jamie were neither of those things.

Walking into Tess's studio without her had made him feel like the worst kind of stalker. The studio was basically one large room with a kitchenette in one corner and a door to the bathroom in the back. A large clawfoot bathtub sat in a corner of the bedroom, separate from the actual bathroom, which had a functional shower—Damien had to assume the people who'd had the studio built hadn't been able to fit the bathtub in the bathroom, so they'd placed it in the bedroom—a curious design choice at best.

She kept the studio as neat as a pin. She'd asked him permission to set up string lights across the ceiling, over the bed and bathtub, and had set up a large desk next to the largest windows, facing into the yard.

This was where she wrote all day every day, whenever she wasn't with Jamie. She'd never shared her writing with him—they didn't have that kind of relationship—but Damien had bought a book of short stories she'd published in university shortly before her arrival. The small volume was hidden upstairs in a drawer by his bedside. He didn't read much fiction, but her writing had taken his breath away.

Sometimes he wondered what Tess was doing in Chamonix—he paid a very fair salary, but it was still a nanny position, and with her writing talent he was pretty certain she could make much more in any other job. Most of the time, he was just grateful she'd decided to join them.

He'd found an oversized sweatshirt draped over her writing chair and grabbed it, along with her pillowcase, stuffing it in the paper bag that now sat by his feet.

"We're going to find them, Damien," Drake said, finally breaking the silence. "You have to believe that."

Damien nodded. That belief, that no matter what, he and his team would find Jamie and Tess, had kept him sane through the night.

As they pulled into the parking lot next to the bakery at 4:45 a.m., Damien heard a dog barking. He recognized the bark an instant before he saw his whole team, huddled together around the front bonnet of a car, studying a map laid out in front of them.

"Everybody's up here already," Damien muttered. He blinked away the tears that sprung, unbidden, to his eyes.

Dawn was still an hour away, so most of his team had a headlamp strapped to his or her forehead. There was Hiro, with Bailey standing by his side. Beside him stood Gael, wearing a backpack that seemed too large for his slim frame but that Damien knew the man could run a marathon in, and Kat, looking almost delicate in her technical clothes, when

Damien knew she was anything but. And finally Jens, who fiddled with the straps of a gray backpack marked with the universal red cross emblem.

They stopped to look at him and said soft hellos. None of them needed to say anything else—the fact that they were here, still in the middle of the night, was enough for him. He wanted to tell them they should wait a little longer—it wasn't safe to search in the dark—but he wasn't strong enough to do that.

Drake took over where Damien couldn't—not today.

"We're going to start the search now," Drake said. "We'll regroup in an hour's time when the Annecy team gets here. Hiro—is Bailey ready?"

Hiro nodded, his eyes narrowed, and took the paper bag from Damien's hands. In the artificial lighting the man's skin looked almost golden.

Hiro kneeled beside the Dutch shepherd and whistled sharply. Bailey cocked her head at her handler—her tongue came out, bright and pink in the darkness. Once Hiro was sure he had the dog's attention, he brought out the boy's stuffed animal and presented it to Bailey.

"Find," Hiro commanded softly.

Damien held his breath. His hands clenched into fists by his side. Search and rescue dogs were amazing creatures, but they weren't miracle workers. Bailey might find nothing, and they needed to be ready for that. *He* needed to be ready for that.

After a brief interlude, however, Bailey barked twice and took off in the direction of the church, only stopping to make sure Hiro was following.

Drake nodded, his expression animated. "There's several hiking paths heading in that direction."

"Let's focus on the ones a six-year-old could have attempted," Kat reminded them.

Damien nodded. Tess wouldn't have taken Jamie anywhere the boy wouldn't have been able to reach comfortably.

"We'll split up in two groups," Drake said, "starting with these trails Bailey has marked out for us. I want everyone in close radio contact. Damien, Hiro, Bailey and I will take the trail up past the waterfall. Kat, Gael and Jens will take this other path. Keep your headlamps on until dawn."

Damien breathed a sigh of relief. It was exactly what he would have done—send Hiro and Bailey in one group, and Gael, who was their best tracker, in the other one.

I'm the weak link in this search.

That's why Drake wants me close.

#

Damien's heart beat hard against his chest. A little earlier, soon after passing the waterfall, Bailey had issued a single bark—her alert—at something on the ground. Although the sky was beginning to lighten, the light was thin enough that they might have missed it, had Bailey not been with them.

Damien clutched the yellow Lego bit in his palm. There was no doubt in his mind that Jamie had dropped it.

He dropped it for me to find it.

I'm coming, Jamie.

Daddy's coming.

Since that moment, they'd found two other Lego pieces—one brown, one white—enough that it could no longer be excused as a coincidence.

Of course, Damien also remembered reading *Hansel and Gretel* to his son just last week.

"We're on the right trail," Drake barked on the phone with the leader of the Annecy team. "Get your pilot to circle the area, Beau."

"Something happened to them," Damien said. "Tess would never have asked Jamie to walk this far."

Drake and Hiro looked at each other but said nothing. Suddenly, Bailey started barking. Her nose pointed down river.

"The Lego pieces are leading us up the mountain," Damien said doubtfully. "We can't stop now."

"Is it possible they split up?" Drake asked.

"Bailey's following your son's scent. I don't know who went up the mountain, but your son went this way, Damien," Hiro said.

"Call the other team, Drake. Get them up here to explore this path," Damien said firmly. "We follow Bailey."

Hiro let out a relieved sigh.

Five minutes later, Damien's heart almost stopped as he saw two familiar shapes running on the far side of the river.

They're alive.

Thank you, God.

The relief was so intense it threatened to bring him to his knees—until he realized Tess and Jamie were running too hard, and getting too close to the edge.

"I see them!" he shouted to Drake and Hiro, who were standing slightly upstream from him.

Damien shouted their names but neither of them seemed to hear him over the roaring of the river.

"Jamie! Son!"

At the last instant Tess put out her hand to stop Jamie, but the boy had too much momentum, and he fell into the water with a splash.

Damien felt himself grow cold. Late July might be the height of summer, but the water up here rarely reached over 37°F. Nobody could spend much time in that water without a dry suit and expect to survive—certainly not a little boy.

He saw how fast the water was moving around them. They weren't far from the falls.

"Fuck!" Damien shouted. The escarpment on his side of the river made it impossible for him to get to the water from where he was standing.

A moment later, there was a second splash. Damien looked up to see Tess land in the water with a controlled jump.

She went in after Jamie.

Tess was a strong swimmer—Damien knew she swam countless laps in the indoor pool every week. She was using that muscle memory now, her arms digging in hard against the water as she angled her body towards Jamie.

Damien could only watch as Tess finally reached his son, grabbing him by the scruff of the neck and pulling him towards her.

"Swim towards us, Tess!" Damien shouted, running parallel to the river. He needed to get further ahead of them before he could help.

Suddenly, a third shape jumped in the water. It was Bailey, who'd jumped right off the ridge and was swimming hard towards Jamie and Tess. In her mouth, the dog carried a piece of rope.

"Find them, Bailey!" Hiro shouted encouragingly over the roaring river. He'd wrapped the other end of the rope against his wrist several times. "Give Tess the rope."

Bailey reached Tess just as the current got stronger. Without loosening her hold on Jamie, Tess grabbed the rope with one hand, wrapping the looped end around the boy's midsection, under his armpits. She held on to the boy for dear life. Behind them, Bailey swam hard.

While this was happening, Hiro and Drake made their way down the scarped terrain. They stood ankle-deep in the water and started reeling in the rescues. With the two men pulling hard, Tess and Jamie were instants away from safety.

Yes.

Thank God.

Damien stood in place further downstream, his hands clenched as he debated between staying where he was and going to his family.

His family.

He saw the floating tree trunk an instant before it slammed into Tess's body. She lost her hold on the rope and slipped away.

No!

Hiro and Damien didn't falter—they kept pulling hard on the rope until, instants later, Jamie was in Hiro's arms. Bailey was there too, licking the boy's hands.

"We have him!" Drake shouted.

His son was safe. Damien wanted to weep with relief, except Tess was still in the water, being tossed around by the current like a rag doll. She'd be floating by in a second, and

56

Damien knew exactly where she was heading—down to the waterfall.

He didn't hesitate—if he waited, Damien knew he could lose Tess to the river.

"Stay with him!" Damien shouted, not taking his eyes off Tess's form. Damien had been swimming in this area before and knew the water was deep, but still felt a moment of fear as he dove cleanly into the water—a rock or log in the wrong place could easily incapacitate him. He kept the dive as shallow as possible and resurfaced quickly, just below the area where he expected Tess to be.

Though he'd expected the water to be cold, the temperature was still a shock to his system. Damien's mind instantly wandered to Jamie, but he pulled himself back firmly—Drake and Hiro would take care of his son.

An instant later, his hand grabbed on to Tess's hair. She was moving so fast he almost missed her, but managed to grab on and pull hard on her ponytail. He avoided her flailing limbs and grabbed on to her jacket, steadying her as best he could in the moving current. He reached under her arms, grasping her shoulders firmly and leaning her back against his chest.

"Damien—" she gasped. She was hyperventilating, whether from fear or cold, now wasn't the time to ask. She was trying to kick, but her movements were sluggish and uncoordinated.

I need to get her out of the water.

Damien swam hard towards the river bank—he knew how close they were to the falls and knew also that the best way to survive a plunge down a waterfall was to avoid falling in the first place.

He fought against the current with all his might—every inch he advanced was one more moment he and Tess had— but the river was too strong and he felt them moving inexorably towards the waterfall.

If he were honest with himself, a part of him had already known this, even as he dove in the water, hence why he hadn't taken off his waterproof backpack before jumping in.

We're not going to make it.

We're going to go over the edge.

It was time to stop swimming and start planning. Damien was calm as he tightened his hold on Tess, locking his arms around her. Her head was a welcome weight against his chest.

"I've got you, Tess," he whispered, tucking his chin into his neck. "Take a deep breath," he asked, though he wasn't sure she heard him over the roaring sound of the water.

Within moments they were swept over the enormous waterfall, vanishing into a cloud of mist that sprayed their eyes and face.

Damien pressed his legs and feet together—they needed to go down feet first. He knew their best chance of survival was falling cleanly into the water where the fall broke the surface tension, making for a softer landing for them— otherwise a fall from this height would feel like landing on concrete.

He heard Tess's scream as they fell—he wanted to tell her again to hold her breath, but there was no time to talk, no time to do anything except hold on to her tight enough that she'd be bruised the next day.

If there is a next day.

Their combined mass landed in the water—hard. Something slammed onto his shoulder, wrenching the bone out of its socket. The pain was instant and blinding, and it was only his experience and discipline that stopped him from screaming out loud and filling his lungs with water.

Tess struggled in his hold, fighting to get to the surface. He held on to her with his good arm—his other arm trailing limp and useless behind them.

Hating himself for causing her fear, he tightened his grasp on her chest and kicked hard with his legs, keeping her underwater—they needed to get away from the falls before surfacing, or else they'd go right under again. Finally, when he deemed they were safe enough, he pulled her up towards the light.

Damien gasped as they broke the water's surface. He made sure Tess's face was out of the water, frightened by her stillness. She wasn't struggling anymore—she lay limp and cold against his chest. The thought that she might be dead was enough to wrench a sob out of him.

He reached the river bank and dragged her up onto the wet grass, then pulled himself up beside her, clenching his jaw at the pain in his shoulder.

He tilted Tess's face and head backwards. Her mouth opened up, and he unceremoniously reached in with two fingers to make sure her airway was clear.

He put his cheek to her mouth and listened, but he was shivering so badly it was impossible to tell if she was breathing.

Breathe into her mouth.

Damien leaned over her, ready to begin mouth-to-mouth resuscitation, when she suddenly gasped for breath.

Thank you, God.

Damien rolled her expertly to her side. Almost immediately, her slim body heaved, and she breathed out what seemed like an entire lake's worth of water.

He patted her shoulder gently, just to let her know he was there.

"You're okay, Tess, you're okay. I'm right here."

Chapter 6

Tess

"Damien?" she whispered, hating how feeble her voice sounded. She thought she might need to vomit again.

He was kneeling next to her, the spot where his body touched hers the only part of her that didn't feel frozen.

"Don't move, Tess. You're going to be okay."

Ignoring him, she rolled herself to a sitting position. She shivered in the cool breeze.

Shit, I'm cold.

"I'll get you a blanket," he said.

"You jumped in after me," she breathed, amazed.

"You jumped in after Jamie," he retorted. "I'll never be able to thank you enough."

"Jamie!" she said. "Are you sure he's safe?"

Damien nodded. "Drake and Hiro have him. They'll keep him safe and send someone for us. In the meantime, we need to warm you up. That water's not—"

She looked at him uncomprehendingly for a moment until she realized he had no way of knowing everything that had happened to her and Jamie. It seemed like a faraway nightmare even to her, and she'd lived through it.

Damien was struggling to take off his backpack. Something was wrong with his left arm, which hung limply by his side.

"What's wrong with your arm?" she asked.

"It's my shoulder. I must have hit it against a rock on the way down and pulled it out of its socket," he said matter-of-factly. "Not the worst thing that could have happened to us."

She looked back at the waterfall.

"Did we really do that?"

"We did," he said, smiling. "Flew right over."

"Not something I want to try again."

"No, me neither," he agreed. "Shit, this hurts. Can you help me take off my backpack?"

She reached over clumsily, her frozen fingers hesitating on the shoulder strap as she watched him pale.

"Keep going," he said through gritted teeth. "Please."

Once the backpack was on the floor, he opened the side zipper and fished out a Mylar blanket, wrapping her awkwardly inside it with just one hand.

"How did that stay dry?"

Damien clutched his shoulder. His nostrils quaked as he worked on breathing through the pain.

"It's a waterproof backpack. Makes it a bit cumbersome, but it means all the stuff inside is nice and dry."

"Impressive," she said.

A noise behind them had her quaking in fear.

We need to get out of here.

She felt so comfortable with him, she'd almost forgotten the threat.

"We need to go," she said.

"Go? We're not going anywhere. I'll build a fire, and we'll get you warm and dry. Drake and Hiro will send someone for us."

"No. We have to get going. He could be here any minute," she begged.

"*He*?" Damien's expression hardened. "What happened, Tess?"

"We'd just reached the falls a man showed up. This was yesterday afternoon."

It feels like a million years ago.

"He threw my phone into the water, pointed a gun at us and forced us to follow him, all the way to a small hut up the mountain. He locked us in one room and left us there. He threatened—"

Damien's expression had gone hard.

Despite herself, tears started rolling down Tess's cheeks.

"Did he hurt Jamie?" he asked softly. "Did he hurt you?"

"No. He didn't touch Jamie. He slapped me once, when I wouldn't do what he wanted, but he mostly... he left us alone. I heard him leave the hut in the middle of the night. That's when I broke a window, and we started running."

Her eyes went to the bruised knuckles on her right hand. Damien picked up her hand and held it in his own, much larger palm—as if she were precious.

"Jamie's not safe until we get him off the mountain. We need to call your teammates," she insisted.

"Unfortunately my phone wasn't in my backpack," Damien said, patting his sodden pocket.

"Then we need to go now."

63

She shivered, wrapping the blanket tighter around her body.

Damien looked around them, narrowing his eyes. She didn't know whether to feel relieved or worried that he was taking her seriously.

"I agree. We can't stay here. But I'm going to need your help."

"What do you need?"

"I'm going to need you to maneuver my humerus back into position," he said, watching her eyes.

"You're kidding," she hissed. She'd almost failed her A-Level Biology exam because she hadn't been able to complete the frog dissection.

But Damien doesn't know that.

And this may not the time to bring it up.

"I'm not kidding," he said kindly. It didn't escape her notice how tightly he was holding on to his shoulder. "I can't run like this, and I can't protect you. I can feel the muscles spasming—the longer we take to reposition the bone, the more difficult it's going to be."

"Okay," she said, and she realized she meant it. He'd just gone off a cliff for her—she could do anything he needed her to do.

"Okay?"

"Tell me exactly what you need me to do."

"Normally we'd start by icing it, but I think we can skip that step in this case," he joked.

She raised an eyebrow at him.

How can he joke at a moment like this?

"Right. I'm going to lie down, like this," he said, demonstrating. "You're going to grab my hand and pull on

64

my arm slowly. Don't let go, no matter what. You'll probably feel it when the head of the humerus slides back into the socket."

"Probably?" she asked doubtfully.

"Pull until I tell you to stop, Tess," he clarified, holding out his hand.

Tess reached to grab the proffered hand. It was cold, like her own, but somehow still managed to warm her inside.

Damien's hand was powerful, with long fingers, a calloused palm and closely clipped nails. Tess had stared at his manly hands before—at the dinner table or while he played Lego with Jamie—it was part of her fascination with her boss, which she seemed to have no control over.

"You okay, Tess? If you're not okay with this, I can try to—"

Shit. He's in pain, and you're here ogling his hands.

"Tell me something. What happens if I do it wrong?"

"I'll probably scream. Then we'll try again."

"Okay. But I'm not going to break your arm, right?"

"You're not going to break my arm," he confirmed.

"Let's do this, then. One. Two."

Tess braced herself against the ground and started pulling slowly on Damien's hand. She kept her eyes firmly on his face. A muscle ticked behind his jaw but he didn't make a sound.

"You okay?" she gasped. Her half-frozen arm muscles complained but she kept going, knowing if she stopped she'd only be causing him more pain.

"Keep ... going," he begged.

And suddenly, just when she thought she literally couldn't keep going, that her strength was fading, she felt the bone pop back into its socket.

"Fuck," he breathed. "That feels amazing."

"It does?" she asked. She'd never had a dislocated shoulder before.

A small smile played on his lips. "Don't get the wrong idea. I meant the pain is gone. Now, let's get going. We're too exposed out here and we need to warm up."

Tess looked undecided.

"Trust me. It's going to be okay."

"How will your team find us, though? What if it gets dark and—"

She bit her lip to stop herself from sobbing out loud.

"You're safe now, Tess. Jamie's with my team—Drake, Hiro and Bailey will protect him with their life. There's a tracker inside my bag. If I know my team at all, they'll come for us in a matter of hours."

He offered her his right hand and helped her up, wrapping the emergency blanket tighter around her.

#

Damien

Damien didn't like the blue tinge on Tess's lips, or the way she walked so silently, carefully putting one foot in front of another. He needed to get her out of those wet clothes and warmed up.

She might be going into shock.
Where's that fucking cave?

Finally, he glimpsed it, just fifty feet further up the slope. He'd been hiking in this area dozens of time, both for work and on his own when he was younger, and knew the small cave would be a good place to wait for help to arrive.

"Just a few feet further," he said, tightening his hold on her hand.

She nodded faintly but didn't say anything else—hadn't said a word since they'd left the clearing by the waterfall.

He left her sitting by the entrance and walked quickly around the cavern to make sure no animal had decided to call it home. It was completely empty.

He took off his backpack and started looking for the things he was going to need. He set the small Bunsen burner going and started heating some water from his water bottle. He dropped some granules of instant tea and sugar into the pot.

While the drink heated, he brought out an extra Mylar blanket, which he placed on the ground, and spread his unzipped Chilkoot sleeping bag on top. He favored his shoulder, which was still sore.

He turned off the Bunsen burner, not wanting to make the drink too hot for her, and poured half a cup into the lid of the water bottle.

He offered the cup to Tess, who took it in shaking hands. He helped her take a couple sips before she put the cup down again.

"Tess, we need to take off your clothes," he said. She looked at him as he spoke, but her eyes were glassy and her expression didn't change. "Let me help you," he said softly.

She whimpered when he took off the Mylar blanket from around her shoulders, but didn't make any other sound as he started peeling off her wet clothes. He struggled with the zippers, his icy hands not behaving as they should.

"You're clumsy," she whispered. "I didn't think you'd be clumsy in bed—"

"What did you think I'd be like?" he asked, more to keep her talking than anything else. He wasn't about to take anything she said seriously.

Her body felt cold to the touch, but at least she was still shivering. That hopefully meant the hypothermia was mild. Finally she was in her sports bra and underwear—he tried not to pay attention to the way the black cotton clung to her curves.

At that moment, Tess started crying.

"It hurts," she moaned softly.

Fuck the shoulder.

Damien picked her up and carried her to the Mylar blanket he'd spread on the floor, covering her with the sleeping bag.

He quickly took off his own clothes until he was in his boxer shorts and climbed under the sleeping bag with her. He was relieved to find her cold against him—that meant he could help warm her body up.

"What are you doing?" she sniffled. "You're cold."

"Not as cold as you. I'm used to being out in this weather. I'm going to get closer to you now, okay? See if we can get you warmer," he said. He waited for her soft nod of approval before moving his body right against hers, hugging her to him as if he were going to make love to her.

You bastard.

Don't think of that.

Damien held her for several minutes until it seemed to him Tess's shivering might be slowing down.

"I like it when you hold me," she said quietly.

He cradled her head in his hands and kissed the top of her head softly.

I like holding you too.

He didn't say it out loud. In fact, he had to concentrate all his energy on not thinking about her as a woman, when the feel of her, her smell, her touch, all called to him.

She raised her head, her beautiful green eyes connecting with his, and he could read her thoughts as if she were speaking them out loud, maybe because they were his thoughts as well.

"Kiss me," she whispered, inching towards his mouth.

"We can't do this, Tess," he replied, gritting his teeth.

"Why not? I'm single, you're single—"

Let me count the reasons. I'm too old for you. There's Jamie to think about. And you've just had a huge shock to your system—

Then her soft lips were on his, and all other thoughts fled his mind. There was just her and him, and the softness of her lips.

He wasn't strong enough to move away.

He gently pressed his lips against hers, returning the pressure. And when her lips opened up—hesitant but firm—he was overwhelmed by need.

Damien stopped thinking about all the reasons they shouldn't be doing this and let his tongue trace her bottom lip, then slip inside gently. He shuddered as she in turn bit his lip gently. As they explored each other's mouths, the world outside stopped mattering. Damien had never known lust and tenderness could coexist in this way.

Chapter 7

Damien

Damien cradled his son's sleeping form from the car to the house. He'd had trouble letting go of him long enough to place him in the booster seat earlier, and now that the boy had fallen asleep, he wasn't about to wake him up.

"I should go into the office," he told Drake, even as he tightened his hold on Jamie.

"With all due respect, *Commandant*, spend the evening with your family. This isn't a search and rescue operation anymore—it's a kidnapping—and if the teams out there find any trace of the kidnapper, they'll let us know."

Damien nodded with his head, watching as Tess got out of the car. She closed the door quietly behind her. Though she hadn't been asleep in the car, she looked dead on her feet.

"I'll bring Tess and Jamie in tomorrow morning, so they can meet the sketch artist."

Drake lowered his voice so only Damien could hear.

"He's going to be okay, Damien. Back at the river, he said he wasn't scared because he was with Tess, and because he knew you were coming for him."

"In the end it was you, Hiro and Bailey who saved him. Thank you, Drake."

"Of course."

"I mean it."

"You know you don't need to thank me, or any of us."

Damien nodded. Sometimes, words were unnecessary.

He thought back to the moment he'd been reunited with his son—Jamie had been sitting in the back of an ambulance, wearing an oversized jumper, his little legs hanging off the edge of the stretcher. When he'd seen Damien he'd jumped off, run to him as fast as those legs could carry him and jumped straight into his arms. At that moment, Damien hadn't cared about his shoulder, or even that he was tearing up in front of his colleagues.

Then the boy had looked behind them and brought Tess into their hug. For a moment, they'd felt like a family.

But we're not a family.

I need to remember that.

Damien had been the one to break the kiss in the cave—because it was inappropriate, because she was vulnerable, because she deserved better from him. But her taste, her touch, were branded in his brain, and he wondered if he'd ever be able to get her out of his system.

Tess walked past him into the house. She was still wearing large, ill-fitting clothes from among the spares he'd carried in his backpack.

Normally she would have walked along the side of the main house to her studio in the back, but Damien imagined she didn't want to be alone tonight. He too would prefer to monitor her, although the EMT had pronounced her healthy enough.

I'd prefer not to let either of them out of my sight again.

"Sit down," he told Tess. "I'm going to put Jamie to bed first and then I'll make you some dinner."

Ignoring him, Tess padded softly behind him in her socked feet.

Jamie's room was a shock to his system. Looking at the racing car bed, Damien could still remember the grief, the fear that'd filled him the previous night.

Jamie's back. He's safe.

Once again he felt something wet on his cheeks—he rubbed the tears away impatiently with the back of his hand. He forced himself to lay the boy down on the bed and covered him gently with the thin summer duvet. Jamie didn't even stir.

"Thank you," he said softly to Tess, who was still standing by the door. "For protecting him. I don't know what I would have done—"

"You don't have to think about that, Damien," Tess said firmly. She walked into the room and stood beside him. "Jamie was so brave the whole time," she added. Her eyes got a faraway look in them, and Damien knew she was reliving what had happened.

He reached out and grabbed her soft, smooth hand.

Although they'd gone over everything, Damien knew he was going to have to ask more questions—but those could wait until the next morning.

From the small bed, Jamie moaned. "Tess ... Where are you..."

He's speaking in his sleep.

"I'm here, Jamie. I'm right here," she said, leaning over to push a dark lock out of the boy's face.

Jamie stilled again at the sound of her voice, his little form relaxing on the bed.

"Sit down," he said, bringing a chair closer. "before you keel over. I'll go make some food and call you when it's ready."

But of course he didn't—because by the time the pasta was cooked, Tess was asleep on the bed on top of the covers, her arms around Jamie.

Damien looked at the two of them, Jamie with his head of dark hair and Tess with a cloud of blonde hair around her face—hair that normally looked soft and silky, but was now matted and limp, a reminder of everything she'd gone through.

Damien felt a surge of tenderness as he covered Tess with an extra blanket from the closet. He didn't want either of them to ever be cold again.

He rubbed his scratchy chin—he hadn't shaved that morning—feeling every one of the thirty-six hours he'd gone without sleep.

Damn it, I'm crashing.

All thoughts of dinner forgotten, he tiptoed out of the room and made sure all doors and windows were locked, then headed to his own room, where he lay down completely clothed and fell asleep.

Chapter 8

Tess

Tess woke up to the smell of fresh pancakes. She opened her eyes, confused, until she realized she was in Jamie's bed. Beside her, the boy slept on, undisturbed.

She looked down at herself, still wearing what she considered her rescue clothes—the last thing she remembered was Damien telling her to stay here while he cooked dinner.

I must have fallen asleep.

That's embarrassing.

Her bladder felt like it was going to explode. She went to the bathroom next to Jamie's room and took care of business quickly. She looked longingly at the shower, but it'd make more sense to go to her own place and shower there, where she had clothes to get changed into.

As she washed her hands, she looked at her face—then wished she hadn't.

Her matted hair hung in clumps around her pale face. Dark circles under her eyes proclaimed her exhaustion. But more than tired, she looked scared.

She looked at the bruise on her cheek from when the kidnapper had slapped her. It didn't hurt unless she pressed it with her finger, but it was a stark reminder of what could have happened to her and Jamie.

Nothing happened. —

We're both okay.

She felt herself hyperventilating and held on to the sink with both hands. Her mind knew she was safe—that Jamie was safe—but it seemed convincing her body of that was a different matter.

A quiet knock on the door interrupted her internal monologue.

"Tess?"

She held on tighter to the edge of the sink, the porcelain cool under her touch. She didn't want him to see her like this, so weak and pathetic.

"I'm coming in, Tess," he said, opening the door. His penetrating eyes took her in, and she knew he could see right through her.

"Hey," he said softly.

He placed his hands over hers. His fingers gently peeled hers from the edge of the sink.

"I don't know what's wrong with me," she said in a thready voice.

"You went through a lot yesterday. You're going to need time. I'm here to help you. You don't need to do this alone."

She burrowed her face into his chest, delighting in the way his arms came around her, enveloping her in a strong, warm embrace.

"Thank you, Damien."

"Come to the kitchen. I made pancakes."

"I need a shower first," she said. "And some clean clothes." At his doubtful look, she added, "I'll be okay. I'll let you know if I need anything."

Two hours and lots of pancakes later, the three of them were on the way to the station. Tess had seen the *gendarmerie* building on her way into town—it was hard to miss it, right by the Church—but had never been inside Damien's workplace.

She recognized a few of the faces. These were the men and women who'd searched for her and Jamie. If they hadn't found them, who knew if she and Jamie would have made it back.

A tall, athletic woman walked up to them. She nodded at Tess and kneeled beside Jamie.

"I'm Kat," she said. "And you must be Jamie. I'm going to introduce you to a friend of mine, who's a great artist."

Jamie nodded. He seemed excited about meeting the sketch artist, unlike Tess, who was only just realizing how little she'd noticed about their kidnapper.

Once Jamie left, Damien led Tess to an office. He set a glass of water next to her.

"I can't be in here," he said. "I'm too close to you and Jamie—to the case. But I'll be right outside if you need anything."

"You make it sound like an interrogation," she joked feebly. The thought stopped her.

Surely he didn't think—

His eyes went hard. "No. Nobody's thinking that. We just need you to take us through it again. Don't leave any detail out. You never know what will help us catch this bastard."

He swallowed, and his Adam's apple bobbed up and down. The muscles in his neck were tight as guitar cords.

Tess placed her hand on his. She'd been so busy thinking of herself, she hadn't realized how much stress Damien must have been under, and how worried he still was.

"I can do it," she said, with more confidence than she really felt. "Don't worry about me."

And she'd done it. By the time she was done telling the story to the kind-faced police officer, she felt like she'd been put through the wringer. She didn't know if she'd remembered anything relevant. Retelling the story had helped, in a way—it'd made her remember the decisions she'd taken at each point in time—the reasons she'd done what she'd done. She hadn't just been a useless victim out there.

"Are we done here, Jacques?" Damien asked, popping his head into the room.

Tess almost laughed, looking at the one-way mirror lining one wall of the interrogation room. If he'd been right outside, as he told her, he knew perfectly well that they were.

"Where's Jamie?" she asked.

"He finished a while ago. My father's back in town—he took Jamie home."

She nodded, picking up her jacket and handbag. "Come on, I'll take you home."

She shook her head. "I'll walk, if that's okay. I need the exercise, and to clear my head."

He shook his head. "I don't want to scare you, Tess, but until we catch his man, we don't want you and Jamie out alone."

"You think he targeted us on purpose?" It hadn't actually occurred to her, that it hadn't been a case of wrong place, wrong time.

A muscle ticked behind his jaw. "We don't know. We simply don't know."

"I'm sorry I don't remember more. I'm sorry—"

"Don't apologize. If anybody should be apologizing, it's me. For putting you through this." He ran his hand along his dark hair. She wondered if it'd feel soft, like hers, or spiky. She should have taken a chance to feel his hair back in the cave, when they were—

Don't think of that.

It happened.

And then Damien pulled back.

If he's not thinking about it anymore, you shouldn't either.

"Come," he said, opening the door for her. "I'll walk you home. It's time for my lunch break, anyway."

On the way out, she stumbled across Bailey. She remembered the way the dog had braved the current to get the rope to her. She'd probably saved their lives. She raised her eyes to find Hiro, Bailey's handler.

"Is it okay if I pet him?"

"Of course."

"I should have brought you a treat," she said, petting the dog's black head gently. Bailey leaned into her touch. "Is it okay if I get him a treat?"

Hiro nodded, looking serious. The man didn't look like he smiled much. "Of course. Just no sugar, no garlic and no onions. They're bad for her."

She laughed. "I'll remember that. You can count on me, Bailey. Next time we meet I'll have something special for you."

Tess let Damien lead her outside. It was a beautiful late summer morning, the sun was shining, and the town of Chamonix was its usual lively, bustling self. Tourists strolled in and out of tea houses, smoothie bars and shops, going about with their day. Colorful wildflowers hung from most balconies.

Tess felt a moment's apprehension as two tall, loud men approached, speaking loudly to each other in a language she didn't recognize.

I never saw his face. He could be any of these men.

Damien shifted to place himself between her and the men, his arm going around her shoulders protectively.

"It's okay, Tess," he whispered. "I've got you."

She nodded, straightening her shoulders. As nice as his arms felt around her, she couldn't have him thinking she couldn't take care of herself.

"Are you hungry? Would you like to grab some lunch?"

Her heart sped up—for a moment she thought Damien was asking her out on a date. Then she realized he literally meant lunch, and her spirits fell.

"No, thank you. I'll eat something at home. I need to get back to my writing."

Damien nodded tightly, his expression unreadable.

Together, they walked past one of the more fashionable cafés in town. People queued for hours to sit at one of the small tables on the terrace, overlooking Mont Blanc. She'd done that herself when she first arrived—her attention had been riveted not so much by the sight of the highest mountain, but by the ribbons of breathtaking peaks extending in every direction around it.

The crowd sitting there now was composed mainly of chic, fit, older couples—the quintessential Chamonix summer visitor.

Her stomach rumbled. A part of her wished she'd said yes to lunch, but she wasn't about to change her mind now.

They walked the rest of the way in silence.

Chapter 9

Damien

They quickly settled back into some kind of normalcy. Or at least, Tess and Jamie did.

Damien watched both of them carefully. Jamie seemed to have put the incident out of his mind, though he was acting clingier than usual—something to be expected—and he'd had nightmares of a wild moose chasing after him in the mountains. That hadn't happened before.

As for Tess, Damien had caught her locking the front door three times for luck as she and Jamie walked home from the playground, and she sometimes got a faraway look to her face that worried him.

But overall, they were both doing remarkably well. Jamie had gotten a new pair of glasses—these were blue, so Jamie liked them even more than the previous pair. Both Damien and Tess had gotten new cell phones, both of them waterproof this time around.

So everything was back to normal, and Tess and Jamie looked like they were doing okay.

Really, I'm the one having the most trouble.

There'd been no sign of the people who tried to take his son. By the time the teams found the abandoned hut, it'd been wiped clean of any prints. Damien had seen the small room where Tess and Jamie had been locked up—the blanket she'd placed on the windowsill to help their escape. But there'd been no sign of the kidnapper, and nothing that might lead them to him.

There was also no reason for anybody to target his son. He wasn't a rich man—he made a good living, but Chamonix was a town filled with the world's richest people nine months of every twelve—he and his team were downright poor by Chamonix standards.

The Annecy team had investigated Tess as well—something Damien had already done before hiring her—and had found nothing in her past that might make her a target either.

They'd tried to trace all vehicles in the area that day, hoping to strike lucky, but this was still a wild region—perhaps one of the last such areas in Europe. Cameras were few and far between, and they hadn't been able to detect anything unusual.

And so the investigation had stalled.

The other reason life hadn't gone quite back to normal for him, was the time he and Tess had spent together in the cave. Damien kept remembering what she'd looked like standing half-naked in the cave, what she'd felt like when she'd pressed her lips to his. And the kiss—the feel of her tongue against his—he closed his eyes at night and could almost feel her in his arms.

He'd lost count of the number of times he'd jerked off in bed at night thinking about Tess.

I'm an asshole.

It didn't help that he often caught Tess giving him long, soulful looks.

She's attracted to you.

You're attracted to her.

What's the problem?

But he knew what the problem was, of course—and it wasn't even just one problem. She was way too young for him. She worked for him. And, most importantly, Jamie cared for her. Damien couldn't do anything to jeopardize that relationship.

He needed to think with his head—not with his dick.

"You look like you swallowed a frog," an American-sounding voice said. Damien looked up to see his father walk in from the yard—looking at the older man, it was easy to see what he would look like thirty years from now. They were both the same height, with broad, wide shoulders, pronounced cheekbones and a square chin. Only the eyes were different—where his father's eyes were dark, Damien had inherited his mother's bright blue eyes. That, and the hair, since his father's dark hair was now more salt than pepper.

"Dad," Damien acknowledged. He and his father didn't have a great relationship. His mom had been the glue that bound them together, and after she died, it was easy for the two men not to see each other for weeks at a time, even while living in the same small town.

That had changed when Jamie had come into their lives. Damien had watched, amazed, as his stern, slightly absent, father turned almost overnight into a doting grandfather.

Now, not a day went by without his father calling or coming over to spend time with Jamie.

His father leaned on a stool in the kitchen counter.

"What's going on, son?"

Damien pondered how to answer that. His father had been out of town with friends of his when Jamie had disappeared, and by the time he got back Jamie and Tess were back home, so the two men had never spoken about it.

"Jamie's not here. He and Tess went out with the bikes."

John rapped his knuckles on the kitchen counter.

"I know. I saw them as they were leaving. I actually came to see you."

That's new.

Damien walked up to the counter and sat down opposite his father.

"Are you okay, Dad?"

John frowned, making the wrinkles on his face more pronounced. "That's what I should be asking you."

"What do you mean?" Damien asked, trying not to let his impatience show.

"What's going on between you and Tess?"

Damien breathed out.

"Nothing's going on between us. Did she say anything to you?"

"No—but I'm not blind. Anyone can see the two of you haven't been the same since … since the incident. I just want to know what you're going to do about it."

Damien breathed out. This wasn't the way he and his father spoke with each other. They'd never had the conversation about the birds and the bees—John had just expected Damien to figure it out.

And yet, he couldn't find it in himself to lie to his father, either.

"I won't deny my feelings for her, dad. But rest assured, I'm not going to act on them," he said, staring at the older man straight in the eyes.

His father leaned away from him. His lips tightened into a thin line.

"I don't think you understand me."

"Maybe I don't," Damien said slowly.

"Maybe you've come across something that only happens once in a lifetime, and maybe you're letting it slip away from you. Do you think you're the only one looking?"

Damien blinked rapidly.

He thinks I should act on it?

"But I thought you'd—"

"You thought I wouldn't want you to be happy, Damien? Why wouldn't I want for you what your mother and I had together …"

"I don't—"

"You're too old for me to tell you what to do—hell, Jamie is too old for me to tell him what to do—all I'm telling you is, I'm also too old to pick up the pieces of this family if you let this woman slip away."

Damien stared open-mouthed at his father, well and truly out of words.

"I can't risk Jamie getting hurt, Dad. Things have been good between us. A woman would—"

"You're overthinking this, Damien."

Damien bristled at his father's tone.

"So, what would you do?"

"Jesus, Damien, do you really need me to spell it out? Ask her out to dinner. That's how we used to do it in my day, anyway, and I can't imagine things have changed that much. Jamie can come spend the night with me."

And that was how he'd ended up meeting Tess outside as she was putting away the bikes after their bike ride. Her clothes were muddy, her cheeks red with exertion. He took her bike and lifted it easily onto the rack in the garage, then did the same thing with Jamie's smaller one.

"You want to go out for dinner?" she repeated. "Sure. Can you change Jamie while I take a quick shower? I'm a bit—"

Imagining Tess in the shower wasn't what he needed at the moment.

"No," he said, grinding his teeth.

"No?" Her mouth curled into a small smile.

"No. I don't want to take Jamie out to dinner. Just you."

Her teeth tugged uncertainly on her lip. She probably had no idea how sexy it looked. "Just me?"

"And me. You and me. On a date."

"You want to go on a date," she repeated. "With me."

I've lost my touch, if it's taking her this long to understand.

For a dreadful moment, he thought she was going to say no. Then her face broke out into a shiny, beautiful smile. "Yes."

"Yes?"

"I'd like that. I need a shower first, though."

There we go with the shower again.

"Thirty minutes. My dad will come for Jamie."

Damien stood there for a moment as Tess walked away towards her studio. Whatever she chose to wear, her butt couldn't look any finer than it did in those tight leggings she'd worn to go cycling.

Chapter 10

Tess

You think you know someone … and then you realize you don't know them at all.

Tess knew Damien was good-looking. Hell, she'd need to be blind not to admire the way his black polo shirt hugged his wide shoulders or the way those jeans fit around his butt.

And when those blue eyes zoom in on me—call me a goner.

She knew he was brave, and that was before he jumped off a waterfall with her.

She knew he was patient. She'd seen him around Jamie, teaching the boy everything from how to tie his shoelaces to how to build complex Lego structures.

What she hadn't known, was that he could be funny as well. She realized now they'd never, until now, been in a situation where they got to share a drink together and just talk. He'd shared his memories of growing up in a tourist destination—how it'd shocked him to learn that some kids only got to ski one week a year.

"So you were one of those kids who learned to ski before he could walk?" she asked.

Damien smiled confidently. "I'm a *Chamonard* through and through. My friends and I were about sixteen when we first heard someone talk about Chamonix's world-famous *steep skiing*—we'd been skiing our whole lives and had no idea what that was. For us, runs came at many different angles, but it was always just skiing." He shrugged. "Of course, that was a while ago. They probably don't even call it that anymore."

Somehow, they'd started talking about the most embarrassing moments of their life. She'd shared—and she'd blame this one on the wine—that time when she'd bragged to everyone she knew about having a secret admirer, before realizing it was her sister who had a secret admirer. What'd made things even worse was when her sister had tried to cover it up.

Even now, over twelve years later, Tess blushed in mortification when she thought about it.

"So … fair's fair. What's the most embarrassing thing that's ever happened to you?"

His eyes crinkled at the corners.

He's probably never been embarrassed a day in his life.

"I'm not easily embarrassed, to tell you the truth. Like a lot of kids, I was caught masturbating by my mother—that was quite embarrassing, though she was quite cool about it." He paused for a moment. "I wish she'd lived long enough to meet Jamie."

"When did she die?" Tess asked, sobering up.

"Ten years ago. She was too young. I don't think my father has really recovered. What about you? What's your family like? You mentioned a sister."

92

Tess shrugged. "I have a sister who's two years older than me, and a brother who's two years younger. We're just your average English family—the kind who spends every summer together in the south of Spain, competing over whose skin would go redder."

"So, now that you've lived in Chamonix for a while, tell me, is there anything you miss?"

"About the UK, you mean?"

He nodded.

"Well, other than my family, I'd have to say Chamonix has everything I need … except for proper cheddar. French cheese doesn't hold a candle to mature cheddar."

"You do know we have over a thousand cheeses in France?"

She wrinkled her nose. "Sorry, Damien—none of them compare."

"Fair enough. I'll have to trust you on that. What did your family think of you moving to France?"

"They worried a bit. Not so much about France, or about you," she said quickly—though her parents had expressed some concerns about her moving in with a strange family, "more about me becoming a writer. I think they were hoping I'd use my writing skills to go into journalism."

"I have to admit something," he said, and his blue eyes were serious.

Uh oh.

"I read your book of short stories. I ordered it on Amazon before you arrived."

Tess almost spilled her drink. That was literally the last thing she expected him to say.

"So … what did you think?" she asked cautiously, trying to force her heart to slow down. He said he *ordered* it, not that he *read* it.

"I loved the stories. My favorite was the one where a young woman comes to terms with her partner's disappearance."

She blushed. That was her favorite as well.

He read them.

"You're really talented. Is that what you're writing now, more short stories?"

She shook her head. "I'm halfway through my first novel. The short story book didn't really make any money—I suppose that's what worries my family—but it did land me an agent. She's amazing—knows more about writing and publishing fiction than I could hope to learn in a lifetime."

The main course arrived. She'd ordered risotto with artichokes, and it arrived in a beautiful arrangement on a deep, asymmetric plate. That was one thing to be said for Chamonix—even when you ordered the simplest thing on the menu, it always arrived beautifully presented.

"This looks amazing," she said.

Damien looked up from his plate of homemade smoked trout. "This isn't even my favorite place. Next time, I'd like to take you up to the mountains, to an amazing place near the Télécabine de Planpraz. Everything tastes better up there."

Next time.

She liked the thought of that.

At the end of the meal, the server, looking mildly bored, came to inquire if they wanted dessert. Damien deferred to her. And she suddenly realized she was still hungry—just not for dessert.

It was the kind of thing she might have kept to herself in normal circumstances. A young woman waited to be asked. Then she remembered the way she'd felt when she and Jamie had been kidnapped, when she'd suddenly realized tomorrow wasn't guaranteed for any of them.

She wanted Damien, and she knew him well enough by now to know he wasn't going to make a move on her himself.

"I want dessert," she said, blushing at the cliché expression, "but of a different kind."

She placed her small, pale hand on his larger hand, feeling the strength and warmth radiating from him. She wanted those hands on her, and she didn't want to wait any longer.

He opened and closed his mouth but no sound came out.

"I mean it. Take me home, Damien."

His Adam's apple bobbed up and down several times but, to his credit, he wasted no time in signaling the server for the check.

Ten minutes later they were home.

"When is Jamie getting back?" she asked.

"Not until tomorrow morning. He's spending the night with my father."

"Good," she said, smiling.

His hands came up to cup her face.

"God, you're beautiful," he said breathlessly. "Are you sure about this, Tess? You can still say no. You can always say no. It won't affect—"

Even though he was holding her so gently she felt, in the strain of his arms, how much it was costing him to stay in control.

Tess opened the front door and pulled him inside, closing it behind them—some instinct told her she needed to take the initiative here.

"Stop thinking, Damien. Let's make the most of this night. Remember the cave?" she asked.

"I haven't been able to think of anything else for weeks. Just the feel of you in my arms, of your lips on mine—"

His words thrilled her. She wasn't the only one who'd had trouble sleeping, then. She'd brought herself to orgasm plenty of times thinking about Damien, but it just wasn't the same.

He was about to blow her mind—she hoped.

#

Damien
Thinking is not the same as overthinking.

He wanted Tess—more than he'd ever wanted a woman before, if he was honest with himself. But that didn't make this right. She was still too young for him, and she'd been through a stressful situation just som short weeks earlier. He shouldn't be—

She placed her hand flat on his chest, right over his heart. Her eyes were serious, like she was about to impart some piece of wisdom on him.

"I know what I want, Damien. You don't need to protect me from anything—least of all yourself. This is a choice I'm making, and tonight I choose us."

Her words propelled him to action. He brought his hand to his chest, looking for hers—curled his large, calloused palm around her soft one and led her to his bedroom, only just resisting the urge to lift her, caveman-style, in his arms. His shoulder had mostly recovered, but there was no reason to tempt fate.

She closed the door and looked around her. Damien saw the room as someone might who was seeing it for the first time—a room dominated by the king-sized bed that was so large it'd had to be pushed in through the window.

He walked to the bed and lit the soft night-side table, then took a step back towards her.

Tess raised her palm.

"Stop there," she ordered, her voice a husky whisper. "Sit on the bed."

Damien sat. He understood what she was doing—she'd told him this was her choice, and this was her way of showing him.

Standing gracefully on one foot, she took off one strappy sandal, then the other, dropping them on the floor. Next, she took off her sparkly top and stood there, wearing just her bra and tight jeans. The bra was black, lacy, and left little to the imagination. It seemed as if her creamy breasts would pop out if she breathed any deeper.

"Should I keep going?" she asked playfully, her hands on the top button of her jeans.

Damien groaned. "Please."

Without looking away from her, he rearranged his cock through his jeans in an attempt to soothe the pressure.

She laughed and started wriggling out of her tight jeans, revealing light green briefs. The contrast with the black bra made his cock swell further inside his jeans. No amount of rearranging himself was going to take care of that.

"Take the bra off," he begged.

She curled her finger.

"I'll show you more if you show me what you've got," she said huskily.

Damien stood up and walked towards her. Barefoot, she was a full head shorter than him, but he had the feeling that, of the two of them, he was the one more likely to end on his knees.

When he made no move to undress, she took the initiative, her slim fingers making short work of the small buttons on his shirt.

Desire shone bright in her eyes as she pulled the material off his shoulders, and he was glad for all the running and training that kept his body strong.

Then her hands moved to the front of his belt, and he lost all ability to think. His hands moved down to help her, and soon he was standing naked in front of her, his cock growing impossibly large at her perusal.

Something shone in her eyes for a moment, then was gone, but he was watching her too carefully not to recognize it for what it was: uncertainty.

Even as his traitorous body rebelled—his cock wanted closer to her, wanted to be inside her—he held himself at arm's length from her.

"Tess? What is it? You know you can tell me anything, right? Do you want to stop?"

She shook her head firmly.

"Stop being so careful with me. I just … you're very large … but I'm sure you'll—"

He smiled. "I'll fit, Tess, believe me."

He held out a hand to her, and she melted into his embrace. His mouth sought hers, kissed a trail from her lips, all the way down her neck. He moved the bra strap out of the way so he could continue kissing down her body.

Tess's little moan went right to his lower belly.

While he continued kissing her collar-bone, his hands caressed the soft skin of her back. He found the hook of her bra and gently unclasped it, freeing her breasts and exposing them.

Her nipples stood erect, the tips dark pink.

Damien's throat went dry.

Then his mouth was on her breasts—feasting on one, then the other, greedily—driven on by her little moans.

"More, Damien, more," she whispered, her hands reaching up to hold his short-cropped hair.

Damien worried he might never recover control after this, but it was a faraway concern.

He picked her up and carried her to the bed, leaving the bra lying where their bodies had stood moments earlier. He dropped her body unceremoniously on the duvet, admiring the contrast between her creamy skin and the navy surface of his bed.

I'll never be able to look at my bed and not see you here.

The thought was gone as quickly as it'd come.

She flicked her long blond hair out of her face and propped herself up on her elbows.

"I like looking at you," she said.

Damien laughed. "And I like looking at *you*." He kneeled on the bed, approaching her. "How did you know green is my favorite color?" he asked. He pulled it down gently, not wanting to rip the fine material.

"It's okay. You won't hurt me."

Finally, they were both naked. He held her to him, marveling at the way their bodies fit together.

Damien groaned as Tess wrapped her legs around him, bringing his hard length flush against her—right where he needed to be.

He moved his hand between them so he could stroke her gently. She was wet already so his finger slipped in easily.

God, she's tight.

His thumb found her clit and stroked the little nub once, twice, delighting in the little cries that let him know just how she liked to be touched.

His free hand found her breast, tweaking first one nipple and then another between his thumb and forefinger. Her back arched against him, giving him even better access.

His finger continued his ruthless, gentle assault. He added a second finger to the first, stretching her. Her breaths grew shallow.

"More," she panted. He was only too happy to oblige. And then she was coming apart in his arms. Her sex throbbed against his fingers. He swallowed hard, wishing it was his cock inside her.

Finally, she lay limp and still. He caressed her face, her neck, her shoulder, avoiding her more erogenous zones for a moment.

"Damien … that was amazing," she said.

"It was," he agreed, taking in her blushing, sated expression.

He felt a moment of uncertainty.

He'd made her come—she looked happy. Maybe he should let her—

Her soft voice interrupted his thoughts. "I think I could come again."

"Is that so?" he asked. His hand went from her neck to her nipple, pinching it until she gave a little gasp.

"Please tell me you have a condom."

He was already ahead of her there, his long arm reaching into the drawer next to his bed, where a box of condoms sat next to her book. He found what he was looking for and closed the drawer quickly—it was one thing to tell her he'd read her book, another thing for her to realize he kept it next to his bed.

He sheathed himself in one practiced move and lay on top of her. Her legs were open, her knees raised to give him better access.

"Tell me if I hurt you," he said He'd felt how tight she was—it was going to be a tight fit, and he never wanted to hurt her.

"I trust you," she whispered. He guided himself in until just the head of his cock was inside her, then pushed inside slowly—stretching her.

Tess's forehead crinkled and her eyes closed. He stopped all movement. "Open your eyes, Tess, I want to make sure I'm not hurting you."

When she opened her eyes, they were hooded with pleasure. "Keep going, Damien, or I'm the one who's going to hurt you," she said. Her hands tightened against his biceps, and he knew she'd feel his muscles straining to keep the weight of his upper body off her.

Finally he was fully sheathed inside her—the pleasure so strong he feared he might come before they'd even gotten started.

"God, you're going to make me come," he said through clenched teeth. "I don't want to come yet."

"I don't want you to come yet either," she said, her expression solemn. "I want us to come together."

Damien breathed in and out slowly, trying to relax—not a simple task with Tess's small, clever hands running around his chest, his arms, his back.

Finally, when he thought he had enough control back, he started moving, the friction between them delicious. He pulled on one of her legs and she took the hint immediately, lifting both legs so they wrapped around his hips and crossing her ankles to hold herself in place.

The position gave him the perfect access. Damien found a rhythm and pounded into her.

Yes. Yes. Yes.

His climax was arriving fast—he was going to get there long before Tess if he didn't get creative. Still pounding into her, he brought one hand between them—careful to hold his weight off her with his other arm, as he didn't want to crush her—and rubbed her clit lightly in rhythm to his cock.

He felt her reach her peak an instant before he did—he felt her clench around his cock as he emptied himself inside the condom.

His forehead went down to meet hers.

"That was brilliant," she said, smiling.

Indeed.

He didn't want to move but knew that he had to. He sat up, disposed of the condom inside a Kleenex by his bedside table, then lay back down beside her.

"You're beautiful," he said, roaming her naked form. She hadn't moved a muscle since he'd left her.

"I need to pee," she said.

He laughed, pointing her toward his bathroom, enjoying the view as she sauntered off.

Waiting for her to come back, Damien felt a shiver run down his body—this didn't feel like sex. Or it did, but it felt like much more than that as well.

He opened the duvet for her to climb under with him.

"Naked?" she asked.

"I always sleep naked. Is that okay?"

"More than okay. But I can't stay long, alright? Just a quick nap."

Chapter 11

Tess

When Tess opened her eyes again, the room was already bathed in the softest morning light.

Shit.

She'd meant to take a nap but had slept most of the night in Damien's arms instead.

And what arms.

Tess looked at him now. Asleep, he looked younger, but even at rest his strength was evident in every line of his body, from his powerful shoulders and arms, down to his defined chest and stomach muscles.

She could still see faint traces of the bruise on his shoulder. She remembered that horrible moment back in the river when he's asked her to pull on his arm—remembered the grim line of his mouth as she'd done so. He hadn't made a sound, but she knew she'd caused him great pain.

It still amazed her that he'd jumped into the river for her, knowing—as he had—that they were just as likely to go over the edge. She realized he would have done the same for anyone, but the fact remained that, on that day, he'd done it for her.

She sat up and looked around for their clothes, which lay strewn all over the bedroom floor. She made a quick plan for how to get to the different things she needed—she wasn't about to strut out there half-naked.

Just as she finished formulating her plan, Damien stirred. He opened his eyes, and she was amazed once again by their ethereally blue color.

"What are you doing, Tess?" he asked, his voice a husky whisper. "Come back to bed."

She shook her head, covering herself up to her breasts with the duvet. "No way. I'm going to my studio. I don't want Jamie to find me here."

He smiled. "He's with my dad. They're not going to come back at—" he stopped to look at the clock on his bedside table, "five twenty a.m."

"Not going to risk it," she said, sneaking out of the duvet to grab her knickers. "Jamie trusts me."

He sobered up quickly. "He's going to have to know eventually, Tess. You know that, right?"

She shrugged, still searching for her bra. Half-naked was not how she'd planned on having this conversation.

If at all.

Damien was out of the bed. Unlike her, he didn't seem to be looking for his boxer shorts, content to strut around naked. His washboard abs were a work of art—what the French so aptly referred to as *la tablette de chocolat*.

Her eyes went lower, to where his cock hung proud and, it seemed, already half-hard. For a moment, she felt her resolve waver.

Someone's happy to see me.
Maybe we have time for a quickie?

Then she thought of Jamie and sprinted towards the spot where she last remembered seeing her bra.

Damien caught up with her in two steps. His fingers went around her wrist, his hold loose—just tight enough to get her attention.

"I mean it. This wasn't a one-night stand, Tess." His gorgeous mouth frowned in a sweetly uncertain pout. "At least, not for me."

She laughed. "Not for me either, Damien. I just … I think we need some time to see how this works out. We'll need to agree on all sorts of things and—"

"I'll speak with my son. This isn't half as big of a problem as you're making it out to be," he said.

She wanted to believe him.

"I'm going to my room," she said. "Why don't you go back to sleep, Damien, and we can talk in the morning?"

"Sleep?" he complained, his hand coming to grasp his cock. "If I can't have sex with you again, I'm going for a hard run, then a cold shower."

She laughed, putting on her jeans. "Enjoy. I'll be asleep again in my bed in about five minutes."

She was lying, of course. She got as far as putting on her nightshirt and crawling into her own bed before she realized her body smelled of him. She thought of everything they'd done together the night before—then thought of everything she wanted him to do to her.

His words resonated in her mind.

This wasn't a one-night stand for me.

Not for me either, Damien.

Giving up on sleep, she took a long shower—although she walked by the enormous bathtub gracing her bedroom every morning, she'd yet to use it—and dressed in her daily uniform of jean shorts and a short-sleeved top.

Nobody needs to know I spent five minutes choosing my bra and knickers—just in case.

It was still only seven a.m., way too early for Tess to even consider sitting down at her desk to write, so she made herself a cup of Earl Grey and called her sister. It was only six a.m. in London, where Sarah lived, but Tess knew she wouldn't be waking her sister up.

Sarah was one of those people born with a built-in alarm clock. She was up at the crack of dawn every day, rain or shine, usually with a big smile on her face.

Pretty much the opposite of me.

She'd also found a job that suited her perfectly, as a radio host in a show that started every morning at seven a.m.

Sarah answered the phone on the second ring. She sounded breathless, and Tess imagined her walking briskly to the Tube as they spoke.

"Tess? Is everything okay?" Sarah asked sharply.

"Hi Sarah, everything's fine," Tess said quickly. Even though she'd tried to minimize the incident from a few weeks earlier in conversations with her family, her sister knew her too well.

"But you're never awake at this time," Sarah huffed.

"Sorry for the noise, I'm walking to work this morning."

"I figured you'd be on your way to work. Just wanted to chat for a bit."

"You sound too happy. And, you want to chat. At seven in the morning your time?" Sarah's voice went up an octave. "You slept with someone!"

Tess laughed. "So what if I did?"

"Tell me about him, what's he like? Is he French? Is he young? Is he rich? I want to hear all!"

"Well, you kind of know about him already, Sarah."

Sarah groaned loudly on the phone.

"Don't tell me you slept with *him*. The kid's dad? The search and rescue guy? Tess, you know better than that. He's your boss, and he is *old*." She paused dramatically.

Tess shrugged defensively—not that Sarah could see her. "It's not like that."

"So what's it like?" Sarah huffed impatiently.

"I don't know. We haven't figured it out yet. But you'll be the first to know when we do, Sarah, okay?"

Sarah's voice softened slightly. "I don't mean to burst your bubble, Tess. I know you've been lusting over this guy for a long time, and it's no surprise, really, that he's lusting over you as well. I just want you to be careful. How do you know he doesn't sleep with all his nannies?"

"I'm not *his* nanny, Sarah. I'm his son's nanny."

"You know what I mean."

"I do, I do. Listen, I'm not mad at you. I'll be careful, okay?"

"Please do, Tess. I miss you!"

"I miss you too, sis. Have a good day at work."

"You too."

Tess hung up the phone.

She's right.

That was the thing about Sarah—she was almost always right. She also hadn't said anything Tess hadn't thought of herself. Logic dictated she should stop this right now. She had a good thing going here, with her job, with Jamie. Maybe it wasn't too late to go back to the friendly, professional relationship she and Damien had always had.

But something inside her rebelled at the thought. It wasn't just the sex, though that had been spectacular. No—what she felt for Damien went way beyond lust. It wasn't even the fact that he spent his days running around the mountain rescuing people. She actually, genuinely, *liked* him. As a man, as a person, as a father.

A boyish voice interrupted her thoughts.

Jamie!

"Tess?" he said.

Tess opened the door to let him in.

"Hey pumpkin, are you back from your grandpa's already?

"He just dropped me off. Hey, Tess, could I ask you something?"

Tess's heart nearly stopped. Just last week he'd asked her, his big blue eyes staring right into hers, if dying hurt. Tess had thought carefully before replying—it was her policy never to lie to Jamie—but she couldn't help worry about the boy.

"Anything," she said, going down on her knees in front of him so their eyes were level.

"Do you think we could go swimming today, up by the creek?"

Tess kept her expression neutral. Jamie hadn't wanted to go swimming since the incident—she hadn't pushed, knowing he needed to process what had happened in his own time, but hearing him say he wanted to get into the water again filled her with joy. Jamie had been to several sessions with an eminent child psychologist, but Tess hadn't expected the sessions to yield results so quickly.

"Don't worry, Tess," the little boy said quickly. "I'll be with you."

She nodded quickly, swallowing back a sniffle.

"Of course we can go, pumpkin. Let's get some breakfast first and then we'll head out, okay?"

She dropped Damien a quick note to let him know where they were going, knowing he was sure to reach out several times during the day.

#

Damien

"Did you guys have a good time?" Damien asked from where he stood on the kitchen island, slicing some colorful vegetables.

"It was great, Daddy. We spent all morning swimming, ate with our feet in the water, and then went back again."

"I see. You're a regular little merman."

Jamie nodded proudly. "So was Tess. A mermaid. I took care of her."

Damien felt his heart constrict.

"Good job, buddy. Why don't you go wash your hands for dinner? I'm making vegetable lasagna."

Jamie nodded, already running out of the combined living and kitchen area.

As soon as he was out of hearing range, Damien dropped the knife and dried his hands on a kitchen towel.

"How was it?" he asked quietly.

Tess's eyes were shiny with unshed tears.

"He was great, Damien. Swam around all day. We bumped into a couple kids from his school and they played together in the water. It was good."

Damien exhaled, relieved.

"Good. Good. I was worried it'd bring back—"

Tess put her hand on his.

"He's fine. You need to relax."

Damien nodded.

"How about you? Are you okay? You also went through a traumatic experience."

"I'm fine, Damien. We had a brilliant day out there together."

Damien couldn't help but smile at her choice of words.

"Maybe we can have a brilliant night together," he said. He wanted to lift her onto the kitchen counter and ravish her right there, but contented himself with placing a hand on her waist.

"Get off me. Jamie'll be back in a second," she hissed.

"I'll speak with him, I promise."

"Not tonight, Damien. We had a full day—he went swimming for the first time. He doesn't need—"

Damien swallowed an impatient huff. He knew his son—Jamie would be happy for them. They were both responsible adults—they could make sure their relationship didn't affect him. But Damien knew he needed to tread carefully, that he needed to be respectful of Tess's opinion on the matter. And, if he were honest, her desire to shield his son above all else, thrilled him.

"Fine," he finally agreed. "We'll talk about it later, though."

Two hours later, after dinner and multiple story books, Jamie was finally asleep in his bed.

Damien watched Tess as she put away the books they'd read. He walked up to her and handed her the one he was holding in his hand, a story of superhero mice saving their city from a supervillain rat. Tess was a fiend about alphabetical organization, so he knew better than to put the book in the wrong spot.

"Hey. It's our turn now."

Damien held out his hand, waiting for her to take it.

"Are you sure he's asleep?"

"He is." He patted his pocket. "I turned on the child monitor on so we'll hear him if he wakes up." He swallowed thickly. "I missed you all day today."

She smiled her luminous smile. Her eyes locked with his, the pupils huge.

"Come with me to the studio," she said, taking his hand and tugging on it.

"Are you sure?" he asked.

"I lied this morning when I told you I was going to back to sleep. I couldn't stop thinking about you." Her eyes twinkled. "I'd like to show you some of the things I was thinking about."

Damien nearly stumbled in his haste to follow her. All the blood in his brain flew south—he felt himself grow uncomfortably large.

They crossed the yard to her studio. He placed the monitor on her desk so they'd hear it immediately if Jamie woke up.

Tess left the main light off but turned on the string lights instead, which bathed the room in the softest glow. She closed the curtains before moving to stand in front of him.

"So ..." he said.

"Take your clothes off," she demanded.

He smiled cockily and pulled off his navy blue polo shirt. He couldn't avoid clenching his stomach muscles as he did so, delighting in her gasp. "Is that what you were thinking about this morning?"

"Keep going," she said. "And I'll show you what I was thinking about."

#

Tess

Perhaps it was simply that they were on her turf now, or that the pressure of their first time together had disappeared, or just the fact that she knew intuitively that she could trust Damien with all her desires. Whichever it was—or maybe a combination of all three—one thing was clear: she'd never felt so sexy before.

She ran her hand along his broad chest, stopping to tweak his nipple the way she hoped he'd be doing to her soon.

In a matter of seconds, Damien was naked in front of her. His cock was as big as she remembered from the previous night—it stood out long and proud.

"You're wearing too many clothes," he grumbled, and his voice sent a rush of warmth through her core.

She took off her top and her shorts, standing in front of him in her favorite matching bra and knickers.

"Take those off. I want to see all of you."

She was happy she'd taken the time to wax in town just earlier that week—the fortune she'd spent at the beauty parlor seemed totally worth it now.

"Fuck, you're beautiful," he said through clenched teeth. He reached out to touch her, but she moved out of her reach, going to her knees in front of him. She wanted to taste him, and realized there was no reason she should deny herself.

She licked down his smooth, hard length, delighting in his clean, manly smell and taste. Finally, she opened her mouth to take him in.

Damien groaned. His hands went to her hair, and she could feel how much it cost him to stay still and let her lead.

She took her sweet time, taking as much of him as she could into her mouth and using her hand to create the illusion that he was fully inside her.

"Oh my God, Tess. You're going to have to stop that now if you don't want me to embarrass myself."

She pulled off his cock and looked up at him.

"What if I want you to come in my mouth?" she asked.

"I'd like that," he said, pulling her gently back up to her feet, "next time. Now, I want to be inside you."

He picked her up before she had a chance to argue—she grabbed on to his thick, powerful arms to steady herself.

"Tell me you have a condom," he said, suddenly.

"Next to my bed. They're English condoms. Stronger than what you can buy here in France."

"Stronger is good. So we can go at it all night long."

"Like bunnies?" she giggled.

Damien dropped her unceremoniously on the bed. She watched as he sheathed himself in the condom she provided—amazed at how roughly he held himself.

"Now it's my turn," he said. He moved down the bed so his face was by her core, and blew softly on her blond patch of hair.

The tip of Damien's tongue went out to lick her nub with delicious intensity—Tess cried out in pleasure at the sensual assault. She didn't even have a chance to warn him before she came all over his mouth.

"Fuck, you're sexy. I want to feel those muscles clench around my cock," he said.

She was still coming when he started easing himself inside her. He felt impossibly large, and she forced herself to relax, enjoying the feeling of being stretched to the limit of pleasure.

"Are you alright?" he whispered, giving her time to adjust.

She nodded. Every time he moved, it felt better, until she thought she might come again. He slowed down, causing her orgasm to run away from her, and she hissed her displeasure, grabbing on urgently to his arms.

"I need more."

"Patience, little one." He cradled her upper body in his arms and twisted them so she was suddenly on top, straddling him. Her body celebrated the change.

"Take what you need," Damien said. His hands held on to her hips, encouraging her as she began riding him, but he let her set the pace.

A part of her wanted to slow down, to keep this pleasure going, but she was too greedy, and it felt too good to stop.

She closed her eyes as a second orgasm hit her, this one even stronger than when he'd made her come with his mouth. Her core clenched against his cock, driving him over the edge as well and eliciting a ragged groan from him.

After the orgasm, exhaustion overtook her. She leaned to, unable to support her own weight on her tingling limbs, and let him gently ease her to the side. He was still inside her, and the position suddenly felt intensely intimate.

"That was … even more than last time, if that's even possible."

Tess was too tired to do more than nod her agreement. She was asleep before her head properly hit the pillow.

Chapter 12

Tess

The next morning, after dropping Jamie off at camp, Tess walked over to her favorite café. Still feeling deliciously sore between her legs, she sat down at her usual table towards the back of the room—she didn't want to occupy the tables up front, with their view of Mont Blanc, as those were favored by the constant stream of visitors.

The café wasn't the fanciest in Chamonix—she knew better than to walk into one of those, but the coffee was hot and creamy, just the way she liked it, and Shay, the owner was happy to let her stay as long as she wanted and write.

Tess opened her notebook—lined, of course—and kicked off the timer on her cell phone. She'd had to buy a new cell phone, since her old one had never been found, and she was still getting used to it.

She wrote without pause for exactly five minutes—it was a trick her professor had recommended, to keep the blank page syndrome at bay. This way, she started the day with three or four pages of scribbled notes already. Sometimes they were helpful—the kind of thoughts that made her plot move forward or helped her flesh out a challenging

119

character—but even when her mind took her in loops, just the exercise of putting pen to paper helped her relax.

After five minutes the timer beeped gently. Tess reached over to stop it, just as a shadow stepped in front of her table. She looked up to see the policewoman, the one who worked in Damien's team.

"Tess? It's Tess, right?"

Tess scrabbled desperately around her mind, looking for the woman's name.

I know her name. What's her name?

Sensing her distress, the woman smiled. "I'm Kat Barreau," she said. "I'm part of Damien's team."

"Kat ... yes, I remember," Tess said. She knew Kat was one of the people who'd stayed up all night to look for her and Jamie. "You're the pilot."

Kat nodded proudly.

"And I hear you're a writer. Damien speaks highly of you."

"He does?" Tess asked, embarrassed.

How much does she know about Damien and me?

"Not like *that*," Kat said, laughing good naturedly. "He just told us you're a writer."

Am I that transparent?

"Is this your novel?" Kat asked, pointing at the notebook.

"Uh—no—that's on my laptop. This is just how I start the day, with some free writing. It's where you write without stopping for a certain amount of time, just to get the brain working."

"Interesting—I wonder if it only works with books, or if it could help me get my reports done quicker. We write a lot of reports."

Tess shrugged, smiling. It was impossible not to like Kat. "I've never tried, but I don't see why it wouldn't work."

Kat's reddish curls bobbed up and down. "I'll have to try, in that case. Listen, I have to go into the office, but it was good meeting you." She paused for a second. "I get together with a couple women friends once a week—there are too many men already in my life. One of them is a journalist, she writes a monthly column about the books she's been reading. I think you'd like her—why don't you join us next week?"

Tess's mouth opened in surprise. "I'd love that, if you're sure it's okay."

"Of course. Give me your number and I'll share the details, okay?"

After she left, Tess sat there for a while, chewing on the back of her pen and wondering how much Damien had told her colleagues about their relationship. Finally, deciding not to worry about that which she had no control over, she opened her laptop and started writing.

By the time she looked up again, it was almost time to pick Jamie up, and she wanted to stop by the grocery store first.

She picked up her things, leaving her usual large tip on the table as a thank you for letting her sit there all morning, and walked up to the old-fashioned till. Shay, the owner, smiled widely at her.

"So, how was it today? How's the story coming along?"

"Not bad," Tess said, smiling. "I'm still struggling with the middle part, but starting to see the light."

"Good, good. Keep working on it and come back soon."

"Thanks, Shay, see you soon."

Ignoring the large Carrefour, which was typical of the brand's characterless establishments, Tess walked over to the

Sherpa store, a smaller grocery store which carried local produce, and even some English products.

No good cheddar cheese, unfortunately.

As she shopped, she wondered how Damien was doing at work, and whether he'd be coming home early tonight. She wouldn't mind a repeat of the previous evening, once Jamie was in bed.

Chapter 13

Damien

Over the last three weeks, they'd had sex in every position imaginable.

Damien had never stopped to consider whether he was an adventurous lover, but being with Tess made him want to explore limits—it made him want to give her all the pleasure imaginable.

He still hadn't spoken to his son about him and Tess—not because he felt any differently about her, but because he wanted to wait until Tess was ready to share their relationship with his son. He'd decided it was something they should do together.

And Tess isn't sure enough of us yet.

He sighed. He knew he needed to give her time.

They'd found a kind of routine, if it could be called that. She spent her days with his son, or writing her book when Jamie was at summer camp, and Damien spent his days at work and, on his down time, thinking about the next time he'd be able to hold Tess in his arms and sink himself inside her. At night, once Jamie was asleep, they got together.

But it wasn't just the sex he craved, and this was harder for him to admit to himself—it was Tess as a person. She made him want to share everything with her—bits of himself that he'd never shared with anyone before and that, ever since becoming aware of Jamie's existence, he'd never thought he'd have the chance to share.

"*Commandant?*"

Damien shook himself back into the present, looking up at Jens as they walked together up the hill. Gael walked behind them, complaining incessantly about the heat, while Hiro and Bailey closed the group.

"I'm sorry, Jens, I was distracted," Damien said apologetically. "What did you say?"

"I was saying, we're getting close. There, under those trees," he said.

Damien sped up. A couple hour earlier, they'd received the call from two trekkers, regarding a man they'd met on their way down the mountain. He was conscious and articulate, and had asked them for nothing, but something about him, and they had trouble explaining what it was, had them worried.

The couple had seemed earnest, and he and his team were sitting around the office anyway, so they'd come up to check it out. They'd driven further than normal hikers could drive, leaving their vehicle close by in case and extraction was necessary.

Damien looked around at the peaks of Mont Blanc rising all around them—the view from this spot was majestic.

He and his team rarely came up this way. This was one of the easy hikes by Chamonix standards—one of those day hikes for children or people who were nowhere near ready to

124

climb Mont Blanc. The hikes were clearly marked, well maintained by the local authorities, and visited frequently both by individuals and by groups led by local guides.

It was rare for them to have to come up this way, and when they did, it was usually a case of a sprained ankle or knee, in which case Kat brought them down the mountain in the helo.

Less than a hundred feet later they saw the figure, slumped over a rock. As they approached, they confirmed his description matched the description the hikers had made of him, down to his flashy striped technical backpack.

Complete overkill for this trail.

"Sir?" Damien asked, raising his voice. "Are you okay?"

The man raised his eyes to look at them. He was younger than they'd originally thought, probably in his late thirties. Slightly overweight—somebody whose day-to-day included little physical activity. At first glance he seemed uninjured, but Damien had seen enough over the years to not make any such assumptions.

"My name is Damien Gray, we're from the *Peloton de Gendarmerie de Haute Montagne*. We're here to assist you if you need help, sir."

"I need nothing from you," the man said gruffly, accompanying his words with a dismissive wave of his hand. He went back to looking at his cell phone. He had an accent that Damien was having trouble placing.

Maybe Russian?

Damien called on all his training as a civil servant to swallow the response that came naturally to him.

As if reading his mind, Jens took a step forward, kneeling beside the man. His medical kit was already in his hands

Jens kneeled beside the man. "What's your name, sir? Let me take your pulse. Sometimes the altitude can affect us and we don't realize—"

The man shook him aside. "I'm absolutely fine. I'm just not having fun. This isn't what the travel agency promised," he said petulantly.

Damien and Jens exchanged a quick look.

Was he serious?

If the man wasn't disposed to let them examine him, there wasn't much they could do.

"Unless you have a helicopter?" the man asked, his beady eyes coming to rest on them. "I have money. Lots of money."

"Uh ... no helicopter, sir," Jens continued politely. "But if you need assistance—"

"That's exactly what I need. I need assistance. I've already called my travel agent. He's going to get somebody to come and find me. But you're here now—"

"Let me stop you right there, sir. That's not how it works—we're not a taxi service. And if you're waiting for a taxi service to come pick you up here, you're going to be waiting a long time—I don't care what your travel agent says."

"Get out of my way, then," the man growled. Standing beside Hiro, Bailey growled back. Hiro's hand came to rest on her head, his touch calm but firm. Bailey settled down.

You don't like him either, do you, Bailey?

The man's phone rang, and he picked it up as if they weren't standing right in front of him. "Yes. What do you have for me?"

Damien nodded to his team, then spoke up again louder so the man could hear him over his phone conversation.

126

"We'll be on our way now, sir. If you need anything, please call 112. We'll be happy to speak, if we're not busy attending an actual emergency."

And with that he turned around and started down the road, leaving the man shouting obscenities into his phone.

"Do you know who that was?" Gael asked, looking up from his phone.

"An asshole," Jens replied quietly. Damien hid a smile. Jens never used that kind of language, either in English or in his native German language.

"Yes, but what kind of asshole?" Gael insisted, turning his phone around so they could see the screen. On it was a picture of a man—clearly their friendly tourist, albeit elegantly photoshopped to disguise the double chin and the lightly protruding belly. "A rich asshole."

"I don't recognize him," Hiro said.

"You wouldn't, unless you were Russian."

Damien groaned. "Please tell me he's not a politician," he said, thinking about the shit that could rain on him from above.

"Not quite that bad. He's a billionaire—he owns hotels and shopping centers, but what he really likes is funding startups. He's the investment arm behind three unicorns, all of them in the cryptocurrency world."

"Shit. That's worse than a politician."

"Get ready for a late night, *Commandant*," Gael said lightly. "The rest of us are going to Stella's bar tonight."

"I'll give the Colonel a heads up, assuming he hasn't already heard about our brief encounter, then head out to meet you guys. I think I need a beer."

"For what it's worth, *Commandant*, I think you did the right thing," Jens said quietly.

Yeah. Let's see how far that excuse gets me.

#

As it turned out, the Colonel *had* already heard about their encounter with the Russian billionaire. When Damien arrived in his office, his boss was sitting on his chair. Nobody knew if Colonel Pelegrin was completely bald, since he'd been shaving his head for a good twenty years.

"Do you like this chair, Damien?" Colonel Pelegrin asked.

Damien sighed, standing at attention.

"I do, Colonel," he replied.

"Good. Try to remember how much you like it, next time you and your team choose to leave a VIP stranded on the mountain."

"Yes, Sir."

The man relaxed, and a small smile curved the top of his mouth.

"Now, tell me what *really* happened," he said.

"We heard a man might need assistance, so we headed up to check. He was sitting there, not injured, but told us he wanted a ride down. It was my decision to leave him there. I told him we're not a taxi service—we're not, right, Colonel?"

The colonel laughed. "You're correct about that, but it's also not our job to piss VIPs off. I got a call from Paris, Gray. Do you know how much I hate calls from Paris?"

Damien nodded politely. He was smart enough to recognize a rhetorical question when he saw one.

"Colonel, he wasn't hurt. He wasn't lost. He didn't need our help. He demanded a ride down the mountain because he wasn't *having fun*."

Colonel Pelegrin's mouth turned into a thin line. Damien smiled inside—*fun* wasn't a concept the colonel put much stock in.

"I'll take care of this, Gray. Just make sure I don't get any more calls from Paris," the colonel said, standing up and moving to the door.

"Uh … Colonel, is he still up there?"

Although Damien didn't want to spend a second longer with that man, a night in the mountains could be dangerous for those not trained or equipped for it, even in the height of summer.

The colonel shook his head, his hand on the doorknob.

"He wasn't happy, but he walked in the end."

The smile was still on his face when Damien walked into Stella's twenty minutes later. Stella's was a small bar, its half-hidden entrance located up a steep slope. In a town devoted to feeding and watering high-net-worth visitors, this was one of the few bars frequented solely by the locals, something that was reflected in its prices as well.

Damien looked at his watch—Tess would probably be putting Jamie to bed just about now. Damien had come by car, so he'd allow himself one beer before going home to them.

He found his team sitting in a table in the corner. They were still wearing their uniforms. Drake sat closest to the wall, nursing an ice tea—Damien knew the man didn't drink, though they'd never discussed the reason. Beside him, Kat was almost done with her beer. She might look slim, but that woman could drink any of them under the table—they joked about the Russian genes that must be hiding in her French family tree. On the opposite side, Jens and Gael were engaged in some intense discussion about the temperature beer should be served at.

Hiro was the only one who hadn't shown. Damien would bet good money he'd made some excuse to go home with Bailey.

There was an empty seat on the end that Damien knew they'd reserved for him, though the bar wasn't that busy tonight.

"You made it, *jefe*. How's the billionaire doing?"

"He walked down by himself in the end," Damien said quietly, trying not to gloat.

"And we all still have a job?" Drake asked. His gray eyes shone with amusement. The others had clearly gotten him up to speed on what happened. "I heard down the grapevine that the colonel visited your office tonight."

"We still have a job," Damien confirmed.

His team members clinked their glasses in a celebratory manner, dragging a smile out of Damien.

Damien walked up to the bar to get himself a drink. Stella's was like a traditional pub that way—they expected you to order at the counter and pay for each drink before taking it with you.

There was a woman sitting alone at the bar. Damien didn't pay her much attention until she turned to look at him.

I'll be damned.

She was beautiful in an ethereal, almost unreal way. He would blame it on the alcohol, except he hadn't even gotten his beer yet.

Her eyes were a soft caramel color, her face framed by the highest cheekbones, her lips bold and luscious, painted in the deepest red imaginable. But it was the symmetry of her proportions that was striking, and it wasn't just her face—even sitting down, Damien could see she had a perfect hourglass figure.

Fuck me.

He turned his attention back to the barman—he really wanted that drink—but could feel the woman staring at him.

"Can I get you a drink?" he asked, without looking at her.

"That'd be nice. White wine, please." Her accent was pure Queen's English.

"And a glass of white wine for the lady, John," Damien said.

Damien turned back to look at the woman. She got off the stool and walked towards him. Since he wasn't blind, this was his chance to confirm that her figure was, indeed, as fine as he'd presumed.

"I'm Lilibeth."

"Damien Gray," he said.

She nodded at his uniform jacket. "Are you and your friends police?"

He nodded, tapping the pads of his fingers lightly on the bar while he waited for his drink. When John finally came back, he carried a glass of wine, but there was still no sign of Damien's beer.

"Cheers," she said, raising her wine glass and sniffing at the contents delicately.

"Enjoy."

"Thanks for the drink. How could I repay you?" she asked, and it was impossible to miss the innuendo in her voice.

"You really don't need to repay me," Damien said. He blushed as he saw Kat staring at him from their table. She looked shocked and, if he were to be honest, slightly disgusted.

I've let this go too far.

"But I'll bet you don't buy drinks for all the ladies you meet," she said. Her long, pale finger rubbed the rim of the glass in a sensual, hypnotic way.

"Listen ... Lilibeth, I need to tell you—"

"No, you listen to me. I like you, and I'd like to go home now. What do you say, soldier? Want to go home together?"

"I'm not a soldier," he said.

"Sorry," she said. "Lieutenant? Captain? I'm just here for a couple of days, on holiday—I'm not familiar with the right terminology. But I'm a fast learner," she said. Her small tongue came out to wet her lips, making them glisten.

Damien fought a short battle with himself, but the temptation was too strong.

"Come with me," he whispered. "I'll take you home."

Something dark flashed in Lilibeth's eyes for an instant— so quick he might have not noticed if he hadn't been staring right into them—then they went back to their soft caramel color.

"My place or yours?" she asked, her voice very soft.

"My place," he said, still unable to help himself.

Fuck, she's going to be pissed at me.

132

"Forget the beer," he said to the bartender, dropping some cash on the counter. Then to the woman, he said, "Give me a second."

Damien went over to his teammates and apologized, saying there was something he had to do. Deep in some discussion about the best mountaineering equipment, they all nodded. All except Kat, whose eyes were smoldering.

"Do you know what you're doing, boss?" she asked, her voice deadly soft. Then, when he didn't react, continued, "What do you think Tess will think about this?"

Shit.

He'd forgotten she and Tess had become friendly in the last few weeks.

"You don't have to worry, Kat."

She shrugged, and he could see in the lines of her neck and shoulders what it cost her to let it go. Finally, she dismissed him and turned to speak to the others.

Damien went back to find Lilibeth, who'd shouldered her extra-large handbag and was standing uncertainly between him and the door. She seemed to have no other luggage. He opened the door for her and she walked outside.

"Am I going to be safe with you?" she asked when they reached their car.

"I'll take care of you. I'm a good driver, Lilibeth."

He waited until she let herself into the passenger's seat, closing the door behind her before walking to his side of the car.

"What will we do when we get to your place?" she asked, her voice a husky whisper.

"Do you really need me to spell it out for you, Lilibeth?" he whispered in her ear.

She nodded, suddenly looking close to tears.

Damien sighed.

He'd taken this too far.

"We'll go in the front door, walk inside ... then I'll probably leave you and Tess to catch up."

He laughed at her stricken expression.

"What?"

"You heard me," he said, his lips curling up into a smile.

"You bastard. You know who I am."

He nodded.

"Though I know you as Sarah, not *Lilibeth*." He emphasized the name she'd given him.

"Lilibeth is my middle name. I don't use it." She paused, her expression somewhere between outraged and amused. "How long have you known?"

"Try since you first approached me."

"How did you know?"

She smoothed her skirt over her long legs. He was bound to notice—he still wasn't blind.

He started the car before replying.

"You were too obvious. You zeroed in on me the moment you saw me, even though I was there with a bunch of good-looking men, most of them closer to your age. A woman who looks like you would have looked at Jens or Gael first—or at Kat, if she swung in that direction. Second, you look like Tess—not exactly the same, she's softer where you've got more edges, but the resemblance is there. And, finally, Tess keeps a picture of both of you on her writing table. Your hair was blonde like hers, back then, not brown like it is now, but you were easy enough to recognize."

Sarah scowled.

"So why did you let me embarrass myself?"

"I apologize," he said, knowing it behooved him to sound contrite. This was Tess's sister—he couldn't afford to have her hate him. "It seemed like fair payback for what you were trying to do to me."

She pondered that one so long he didn't think she was going to reply, but then she finally nodded her agreement, relaxing into the seat beneath her.

"Is it okay if I call you Damien?"

"Of course."

"May I ask you something personal?"

"Go ahead. It seems like we've gotten pretty personal already," he laughed.

"What if you hadn't known it was me?"

He kept his eyes on the road ahead. "Would I have slept with you, you mean?"

"Yes," she said.

"No."

"No? Why not? You don't find me attractive?" she pouted.

He sneaked a quick look at her. "You don't need me to tell you that you were the most beautiful woman in that bar. Hell, you're probably the most beautiful woman in all of Chamonix."

"But you wouldn't have slept with me."

"I wouldn't have slept with you because you're not your sister."

Chapter 14

Tess

Tess heard the front lock engage. She wasn't worried — Chamonix was one of the safest towns in the world, plus something told her it would be particularly idiotic to try to rob a policeman's home.

She was surprised Damien was coming home so early. He'd called her on his way out of the office just a short while ago, said he was going to meet his team members for a drink at Stella's.

Tess liked that bar. She liked everything about Chamonix, particularly the things she got to experience as a local, rather than a tourist. There was so much tourists missed about the little town. They spent more of their time in the main street, with its flashy designer stores and overpriced restaurants, but Chamonix was so much more than that.

The door opened and Damien came in, followed by someone else. Tess's first instinct was to run — she was wearing jogging shorts and a ragged, old sweatshirt she never wore outside the house — she didn't want to meet any of his friends dressed like this. Then she recognized the figure behind him and stopped in her tracks.

"Sarah?" she stammered.

Her sister couldn't be here.

"Tess!"

Sarah stepped out from behind Damien and ran to her, enveloping her in a hug.

"Sarah!" Tess squealed. "You're really here."

It'd been close to six months since she'd seen anybody from her family, and to see Sarah here now, so suddenly, was overwhelming. Tess hugged her back, blinking back some tears.

"What are you doing here?"

"I came to visit my little sister, of course."

"But your job, you—"

"I was on my way to Paris for a radio show. I should have been there tonight, but told them there was something important I needed to do. I'm leaving tomorrow evening. You look great, Tess," Sarah said.

"Not as great as you do," Tess laughed. There'd never been a competition between them where looks were concerned—or if there had, she and Sarah wouldn't have even entered the same race.

Where Tess had often been told she was cute, maybe even pretty, Sarah was out of this world beautiful. Perhaps that's why she had decided to make the radio her profession—so people would stop talking about her looks, and would finally realize that she was much more than her appearance.

"We have so much to catch up on," Tess said, taking her sister's hand. Then she realized Damien was still standing there.

"Damien. Thank you. How did you—"

He shook his head quickly. "I can't take any credit for this. I met her at the bar," Damien said lightly, "and brought her home."

A look passed between them that Tess couldn't interpret—she'd have to ask Sarah about it later.

"You two probably have a lot of catching up to do. I have to get up early, so I'll say goodnight now."

As he walked by her, Tess reached over and took his hand in his.

"Thank you," she whispered.

Damien surprised her by raising her hand to his lips and kissing it gently. Though it was a light kiss, she felt it all the way up her spine. For a moment, she forgot all about Sarah, until Damien's words brought her back.

"Spend time with your sister," he said. "I'll take care of breakfast in the morning and call my dad to take Jamie for the day."

"No, don't be silly. Sarah and I will drop him off at summer camp in the morning and pick him up for lunch. We'll have fun together."

Damien cocked his eyebrow at her. "Okay. If you're sure," he said, giving her hand a last squeeze.

I love you.

Where did that thought come from?

For a moment she feared she'd spoken out loud but when neither Damien nor Sarah reacted, she relaxed.

She wasn't in a position to think, let alone say, something like that. In fact, where he'd at first been so vocal that they should tell Jamie about their relationship, lately he'd stopped insisting. Tess wasn't sure what to think about that—was he waiting for her to say something about it, or had he decided that whatever was between them wasn't serious enough to share with Jamie?

The door to Damien's room closed gently, bringing Tess back to the moment. This wasn't the time to think about her and Damien—not when Sarah was standing right in front of her.

"What are you really doing here, Sarah? Is everything okay? Are mom and dad okay?"

Sarah waved a perfectly manicured hand in her direction. "They're both fine. They don't even know I'm here, actually. It was a bit of a last-minute decision."

"So why *are* you here?"

"You want the truth, little sister? I was worried about you. I wanted to check that you were really okay."

Tess's eyes filled with tears again. She blinked at them desperately.

"I'm okay, Sarah," she confirmed.

Sarah nodded, her lips curling into a knowing smile. "I can see that now." Her eyes moved towards the door Damien had disappeared through. "He's hot, your man."

Tess felt herself blushing fiercely.

"He is." She cocked her head—something in Sarah's voice told her she was missing something. "He said you met in a bar. You tried to pick him up, didn't you?" she asked.

Sarah shrugged, not even trying to deny it. They knew each other too well.

"I just wanted to see what he would do. I asked around town, looking for the bar police officers most often frequented, and saw him as he came in. I recognized him from the pictures you'd shared. So I approached him."

"So? Was he tempted?"

Tess already knew from her sister's expression that he hadn't been. Not that she would have expected him to—Damien was honorable to the core, and whatever else might be going on between them, she knew they were exclusive.

"No, he didn't," Sarah confirmed. She paused dramatically. "I like him."

That was high praise coming from Sarah. The last time she'd liked one of Tess's boyfriends was … never.

"Do you really have to leave tomorrow?"

"I do. But you know I don't need much sleep, we can stay up talking half the night, like we used to do," Sarah said, laughing. "You'll let me read what you've been working on?"

Coming from anybody else, the words would have raised Tess's hackles immediately, but Sarah was the one person she'd always shared her work with—her harshest critic, and also the person who'd first convinced Tess of her talent.

"Come, I'll show you were I live."

They settled in her little studio, and Tess immediately put the kettle to boil. Even more so than the average English person, Sarah loved her tea.

"So … you really like him, huh," Sarah began once they were sitting down, each with a steaming mug in front of them.

Tess nodded, then decided to be honest with her sister. "I think I've fallen in love with him, Sarah. I didn't mean to, but—"

Sarah nodded and blew into her mug.

"Before meeting him, I might have worried. Now, not so much anymore." She grinned. "And it's not just because he's so hot."

Tess giggled.

"He is, isn't he? He's really amazing, Sarah. He's great with his son, he's brave and generous and—"

"Okay, okay, I get the point. He's wonderful."

"He is ... and I can't wait for you to meet Jamie as well. He's an amazing kid."

"Yeah, about the kid ..." Sarah began cautiously. "You *do* know what you're getting into?"

Tess nodded.

"Damien and Jamie, they're ... a package deal. I think I've fallen in love with both of them."

"You have to tell Mom and Dad," Sarah said.

"Hold your horses, Sarah. I have to tell him first. He and Jamie have been alone for a long time. I don't know if they're ready for something like this—or if I'm ready."

"Well, you'd better make yourself ready, because I have the feeling Damien feels the same way about you."

"You know you're the best sister a girl could have, and also the best friend, right?"

"Right back at you, little sister. I'll always be here for you. You know that."

"So, tell me about your work," Tess said, changing the topic. "How are things going? Are you seeing someone?"

"Good, and not so good. As in, the job's going great. This program in Paris, it's the first of a monthly series I'm doing in different European capitals. It's a once-in-a-lifetime opportunity. Not so good, because the job doesn't leave much time for anything else. It's not that I want to turn into an old spinster—"

Tess laughed. "A *spinster*? I don't think I've heard that word used out of a Jane Austen novel, Sarah. People don't *become spinsters* anymore."

Sarah nodded thoughtfully. "Perhaps *people* don't, but I'm at real risk of having it happen to me. I'd like to find a man who's not a creep, and who understands how important my work is for me. It wouldn't hurt if he could be as hot as your man's colleagues—they were at the bar earlier tonight and one of them literally made my eyes pop out of my head."

"Which one?"

"I didn't hear his name—didn't want to be too obvious about it, but he was H.O.T."

"Dark hair? Asian-looking? With a beautiful black dog by his side?"

"No—nobody there matching that description. This guy had dark blond hair, tall and muscled. He was speaking English but his accent sounded German."

"That's Jens. He's a doctor. Why didn't you speak with him? Oh, I forgot—you were too busy trying to pick Damien up."

Sarah had the grace to blush. "Yeah. You know me. Work before pleasure always."

"I can introduce you to him tomorrow."

"No, please don't. I'll be leaving soon. It's better this way."

"Okay. If you're sure."

"I'm sure. Now show me what you've been writing!"

Chapter 15

Damien

"My sister liked you," Tess said.

Damien held her tighter. He could feel the sadness pouring off her after having said goodbye to her sister.

"I liked her too," he said. "She's protective of you."

"She's my older sister," Tess said proudly. "I know she tried to pick you up at the bar."

"Did she tell you I wasn't interested?" He grabbed on to her waist and pulled her closer. "That I'm only interested in one woman?"

"She did," Tess confirmed, laughing.

I want to hear her laugh more.

Damien felt a tug on his conscience. "I feel kind of bad. I should have let Sarah know I knew who she was from the moment I lay eyes on her."

"Don't worry about it. I told you she likes you."

Damien went down on one knee to tie his bootlaces.

"I wish we could spend the day together today, but I need to head up to the Majestic—there's a Climate Change event."

"I'm taking Jamie to his friend Xavier's house this afternoon. Apparently he has two pools—an outdoor one and an indoor one."

Damien nodded. Xavier was the son of one of France's top snowboarders. The guy was the face of countless brands. He'd be surprised if they only had two pools in their house.

"Let me cook you dinner, then, when Jamie's in bed. Something spicy."

Tess laughed. "Spicy, huh? You forget I grew up with Friday night curry. You're going to have trouble shocking me."

Damien headed off to work, torn between feelings of happiness, and a nagging worry that this couldn't be real, that at some point the other shoe would drop.

The conference was a small affair—much smaller than Chamonix's conference center, known locally just as the Majestic, could hold. There would be little press and no corporates showing up to make great claims, and for this Damien was glad—just scientists, looking to exchange ideas and make science-based proposals to governments and administrations.

This was a topic close to Damien's heart. He and this team spent all day every day out in the mountains—they were seeing the changes up close, though nowhere was the footprint of climate change more evident than in *Mer de Glace*, their local glacier. Two years ago they'd had to add an extra eighty steps so visitors could get closer to the glacier. If things kept going this way, soon there might be no glacier left for people to visit. It'd become a long-lost memory.

Damien and his team were there to support the local teams and reinforce security, but he couldn't help listening to the scientists' analyses and discussions. As the day went on, he was filled with a sense of dread—not for himself, this time, but rather for Jamie and the children yet to come—the ones who might end up growing in a world so different from this one through no fault of their own.

"Damien Gray," said a voice behind him. Damien turned to see Diana Granger walking towards him. They'd grown up together in Chamonix—it was difficult to predict, back then, that she'd grow up to become one of the world's leading glaciologists.

"Diana!" he said. It'd been years since he'd seen her, but she still looked the same, except for her hair, which she'd dyed a pale silvery color.

"How long are you in town for?"

"Just two days, then I'm going back to Grenoble. They always manage to make these things clash with exam time," she grumbled good-naturedly.

Damien laughed, turning to his team. "Gael, Kat, meet Diana Granger. She is—"

Kat nodded enthusiastically. "We know who you are, Dr. Granger. It's a real honor to meet you." It was strange to see Kat acting like a groupie—she looked seconds away from asking Diana for her autograph.

Gael, on the other hand, was uncharacteristically quiet as he shook Diana's hand. His dark green eyes, so distinctive on his tan, golden face, were hooded.

"Call me Diana, please."

"So no time to head up to the mountains? For the good old days?" Damien asked. He and Diana had spent all their free time when they were children up in the mountains.

Diana looked longingly at the horizon. "I'll take a rain-check on that for sure, Damien. It was good to get the chance to speak. Kat, Gael, it was a pleasure to meet you."

"Wow," Gael finally said, as soon as Diana was out of earshot.

"She's gone, I think you can close your mouth now, Gael," Kat laughed.

"We don't all love the sound of our own voice as much as you do, Miss it's-a-real-honor-to-meet-you," Gael pushed back.

Kat shrugged. "Maybe not. But I know you well enough to know you're rather fond of the sound of *your* own voice. For some reason, Diana Granger just rendered you speechless."

"Come on, guys, I have a kid at home already, don't need some at work as well. Let's get back to the office."

"Can we stop to get some food on the way, *jefe*?" Gael asked.

"It's two p.m. We had lunch less than two hours ago. You're always hungry, Gael," Kat complained.

"Yeah, so? I have a healthy metabolism!"

Damien laughed. "Sure. We can stop."

Ten minutes later they were standing at the famous Chamonix food truck.

"*Frites*, really?" Kat asked.

"You want some?" Gael asked, offering her the cone full of golden fries.

"Nah, I don't have time tonight to run the marathon I'd need to run in order to burn those calories."

"Suit yourself, Kitty Kat," Gael said, stuffing another fry in his mouth. "They're good."

"Gael, if you call me that one more time—"

Gael's green eyes crinkled.

"Relax, I'm just kidding, I'm—"

Gael and Kat's phones started ringing at the same time.

Never a good sign.

It was Kat who picked up first.

"Hello?" A moment later she offered her phone to him, her expression grim. "It's Drake. Something's happened, and you're not picking up."

Chapter 16

Damien

"Drake? What's going on?"

"Where are you, Damien?"

"We're at the Index Bus, Drake. What's going on?"

"You need to come to Place Balmat, Damien."

Damien's hand clenched around the phone so tight the plastic cracked. Place Balmat was right next Jamie's morning summer camp.

"Is Jamie okay?"

"Jamie's fine."

"Is Tess okay?"

Drake took longer to answer this time around.

Please let her be okay.

"She's fine, Damien."

"Drake—"

"She's okay, just shook up. She was on her way to pick Jamie up when a car almost ran her over. She's fine, Damien. That's not the problem."

Damien held his breath, waiting for his friend to continue.

"A few witnesses saw everything, Damien. They claim the car was aiming straight for Tess. This wasn't an accident."

Damien's body shook.

"She's fine," Drake repeated. "She's right here. Let me put her on the phone."

"I'm fine, Damien," Tess said. She sounded out of breath or in pain or scared, or maybe all three at the same time. "I called your dad, and he went to pick Jamie up. Thank God he wasn't with me."

"What happened, Tess?"

"I hardly know, it was all so quick," she replied in a quavering voice. "I was walking on the sidewalk, when suddenly a car appeared out of nowhere. I jumped out of the way but … can you come here, Damien?"

"I'm already on my way. Wait there for me, honey," he said, already moving towards the car.

Kat and Gael followed, all traces of their earlier joking erased from their faces. Damien watched Gael dump the cone with the French fries in a nearby trash can.

Damien hung up the phone and started the ignition, barely waiting for Gael's ass to hit the seat before peeling out of there.

She's okay, she's okay.

But there's no damn way this is a coincidence.

Damien's heart beat hard against his chest.

"Is Tess okay?" asked Kat, who'd been close enough to him to hear part of the conversation.

"I think so—but a car tried to run her over. Once we get there, I'd like you both to take the car and go to my father's house. Stay with Jamie, please, until I get there."

Both nodded quickly. "Of course."

Damien didn't hesitate to flash his lights at other cars, running two red traffic lights in order to get there quicker.

He saw Drake standing there with two other *gendarmes*. Behind them was an ambulance.

Damien left the car keys in the ignition and ran to the ambulance, almost bumping into Tess, who was being helped out of the back of the ambulance by a medic.

Her green eyes stood out from a face a shade paler than usual.

"Tess!"

Damien grabbed her shoulders, enveloping her in a hug. He loosened his hold quickly as she made a soft pained noise.

"Where are you hurt?" he asked.

"Mainly my shoulder," she breathed. "But it's just road rash—don't stop holding me, please."

He noticed now what he should have noticed before crushing her in his arms—her entire right arm was covered in gauze from the hand up to the shoulder.

The medic behind her stepped out of the ambulance. He and Damien had met before. Damien thanked him profusely.

"I cleaned the wound and gave her some antibiotic ointment. I still recommend she gets it checked out at the hospital tomorrow, just to be safe."

"No hospitals," she said. "I want to go home."

A couple minutes later, Tess had signed the necessary release forms, and was discharged. Together, they watched the ambulance drive away.

"What happened, Tess?" Damien asked, hoping his voice didn't sound as shaky as he felt.

"I was thinking about other things, didn't even notice the car as it came around the corner. It's only as it started getting close that I realized just how fast it was going."

"Did you get the license plate number?" he grunted.

Over Tess's shoulder, Drake rolled his eyes.

"Yeah, I wrote it down for you before diving out of the way," Tess snapped.

"I'm sorry," he muttered. "I was just wondering if you noticed anything about the car."

"It was a black car, one of those large Porsches that people seem to be so fond of here."

A Porsche Cayenne.

Anywhere else, that might be an easy car to find. Unfortunately, in Chamonix they were a dime a dozen—both rented and owned.

"I saw one number, a seven. And it was a French plate, if that helps."

"It all helps," Damien said encouragingly. "Did anybody else notice anything about the car?" he asked, looking at Drake.

"*Madame* Riquier was walking her dogs—she saw the entire thing, but unfortunately she wasn't wearing her glasses. She agrees the vehicle was dark."

"Black. It was black," Tess said firmly. "The driver was large—I didn't get a good look at him, just the impression of a large shape behind the wheel."

Damien reached out to remove a twig from her blond hair. He realized his hand was shaking. Tess could have died—again.

He'd been too lax. He'd wanted to believe the kidnapping incident was an isolated incident, that Tess and Jamie had simply been in the wrong place at the wrong time. Damien's hands curled into fists. Someone wanted to hurt his family.

Tess seemed to be thinking the same thing.

"I'm scared, Damien. Normally I would have been walking back with Jamie. It was random luck that he wanted to stay at camp a bit longer with his friends. I told him I'd grab a coffee and pick him up a little bit later." Her upper lip trembled. "I just don't understand why somebody would want to hurt us—"

"Let me take you home, Tess. We'll pick Jamie up along the way."

#

Tess

Tess shivered as she recalled the moment she'd realized the car was coming straight towards her.

She'd been distracted, immersed in her plotting, thinking about the moment her main character finally discovered her father wasn't dead after all. It was going to be a big turning point in the novel, but Tess still had to figure out how to thread it together in a way that wasn't obvious to the reader.

She'd been so busy with that problem, she hadn't seen the car until it was almost too late. She thanked her lucky stars and quick reflexes, as well as the lamp—she'd jumped out of the way like an extra in an action film, except in this case there'd been no soft pad to soften her landing. Just rough, hard tarmac.

She winced as she attempted to move her right arm. Under the bandage, the skin of her arm and shoulder was scraped raw. It felt swollen and tender, a constant reminder of how lucky she'd been to hit the road. A four thousand pound car would have done a lot more damage.

The medic had instructed her to reapply antibiotic ointment that evening, reminded her to check in at the hospital the next day just to be safe, and suggested she take it easy.

Easier said than done.

Tess leaned back in the car seat, struggling unsuccessfully to find a comfortable position.

"Dial John," Damien said. Moments later, Jamie's grandfather's voice came on the car's speaker.

"Tess and I are in the car, Dad. We'll be at your place in fifteen minutes."

"Is Tess okay?" John asked, his voice cautious.

"She's okay. It could have been a lot worse. Is Jamie okay?"

"He's playing with Gael. Why don't you take Tess home and take care of her? I'll bring him by in time for dinner."

"Are you sure?" Damien asked, sounding torn.

"I won't let him out of my sight, Damien," John replied. "And I'll ask Gael and Kat to escort us to yours."

"Thank you, Dad. We'll see you tonight, then."

Tess twisted in her seat, hissing in pain.

"We'll be there soon, Tess," Damien said. His hands were white against the steering wheel.

When they got home, Tess followed Damien to the doorway but didn't go into the main house.

"I'm going to go get changed, if that's okay," she said, pointing to her torn shirt.

"Of course." His eyes were full of concern. "Do you need any help?"

Tess shook her head and walked away. She made it to her little studio, getting so far as to close the white door behind her before collapsing on the wooden floor, her back against the side of the bed.

Her hands shook and tears flowed down her cheeks. She was smart enough to recognize it for what it was, a delayed shock reaction, but that didn't make it any easier to stop herself from shaking.

Her mind was going a hundred miles an hour—she shuddered to think Jamie could have been walking with her. Would she have had the presence of mind—and the reflexes—to shove the boy out of the way? The alternative was unthinkable.

Tess placed her head down against her knees and hugged her legs, for the longest time just sitting there, concentrating on breathing in and out.

She didn't even hear the knock on the door, but suddenly she felt the presence of somebody else in the room.

\#

Damien

Damien never panicked at work—in his fifteen-year career with the PGHM, he'd gained a reputation among his colleagues for level-headedness. It was something he worked hard at, and something he tried to teach all newcomers—you didn't last long in the job if you weren't able to keep your distance.

If they could only see me now.

He certainly wasn't doing a great job at keeping his distance—he couldn't, not when Jamie and Tess were involved.

Even though he knew she was fine, every time he blinked a movie ran in his mind of a large Porsche Cayenne mowing Tess down. In his mind, her slim body flipped onto the hood of the car, slamming onto the large windshield. It was so real he could almost hear her body breaking.

Damien clenched and unclenched his hands.

He walked through the living room and stared at Tess's small studio in the backyard. Nothing moved behind the curtains.

She's probably showering.

But it's been a long time.

Before he could talk himself out of it he was out the patio doors and out on the yard, his long legs easily covering the distance between him and the studio. He knocked softly on her door and waited, counting the seconds.

One Mississippi. Two Mississippi. Three Mississippi.

He got as far as five before he started worrying that something might be wrong.

"Tess?" he asked, knocking again—louder this time.

Where is she?

Damien didn't hesitate to turn the door knob—it wasn't locked. Damien pushed it open cautiously, half expecting her to throw something at him for walking into her space like this.

He had an apology ready on the tip of his tongue, but the words died as soon as he saw her sitting on the floor, her head between her knees. Great, silent sobs racked her body—it was clear she hadn't even heard him come in.

Damien stopped. Fury and fear overtook him. For a moment, he didn't know what to say. Then she looked up at him, fear etched onto her face.

"Tess," he whispered, coming to his knees beside her. His arms wrapped around her, mindful of the bandages on her arm.

"Damien. I'm sorry, I didn't hear you come in. I was just about to—"

He saw her struggling to make something up.

"It's okay," he said. "It's going to be okay. I'm not going to let anybody hurt you."

"I'm not hurt. Not really. I just can't stop thinking about—" Her slim fingers grabbed on to her ruined shirt.

"Let me run a warm bath for you," he said. "We'll keep your arm and shoulder out of the water—you'll feel better afterwards."

Without waiting for an answer, he turned on the faucet and waited for the water to get warm, then added some shower gel. He looked at the light foam, wishing he had the right soap to fix her a proper bubble bath. The thought of Tess's body half-hidden by a cloud of foam made him hard as a rock, but he ignored his traitorous cock.

Not the right time.

Damien helped her take her shirt off. He hissed in a breath as he caught sight of the bandages, which went from her shoulder all the way to her elbow. Her jeans were probably hiding other scrapes and bruises.

He helped her balance on one foot, then on the other, as she pulled off her jeans.

"Let's take these off as well," he said, pulling her panties down reverently. He caught a whiff of a scent that was just her—he wanted nothing more than to lick and suck at her until she came apart in his arms.

This is about Tess

She needs you to take care of her, not ravage her like a wild animal.

But that didn't mean he couldn't look his fill. He loved the way her hips flared out from her slim waist—loved the light blond curls that hid her sensitive nub. And her breasts, beautiful pink-tipped globes—the perfect handful. As he watched, her nipples went hard as ski-pole tips.

Her breathing, too, was ragged. She wasn't unaffected.

"Maybe we can forget the bath, Damien," she whispered.

Even as his cock thickened the voice inside his head got louder.

Take care of her.

"What if I get in with you?" he said.

She looked doubtfully at the tub. "I'd like that," she said shily. "You think we'll both fit?"

He shrugged. He'd never used it, but it seemed like it would fit both of them, if they sat as close as he wanted them to sit.

It's going to be torture to sit in there.

But it's not about you.

Damien took off his dark blue polo neck, jeans and boxer shorts, letting the clothes puddle at his feet, and stepped inside the tub. The water was hot around his feet and shins—almost hotter than could be considered comfortable, though he knew it would cool quickly enough. As he sat down in the hot water, he felt his cock and balls shrivel.

Probably a good thing.

He lay down with his back against one end of the large tub, leaning one knee against each side. In direct contrast with the water, the sides of the porcelain tub were cool.

"Come on, get in," he said, pulling gently on Tess's hand as he helped her over the edge of the tub.

A moment later she was lying against him, her warm back against his chest.

"Mmmm," she moaned softly.

He made sure her right arm and shoulder were out of the water, then relaxed against the back of the tub. The feeling of having Tess in his arms went way beyond sexual pleasure— it was a sense of completeness he'd never realized he was missing.

She moaned again, and Damien caught sight of her pink tongue. He shifted his hips slightly, hoping she couldn't feel his cock responding to the sound.

"I guess I didn't realize how tense I was." When he didn't reply, she spoke again. "Are you okay, Damien?"

He held on tight and lowered his nose to her hair, sniffing her clean scent. "When Drake called me, I was so scared, Tess." His voice broke—a strange, foreign sound.

Tess wriggled in the water, turning her head towards him.

"Hey," she said, her hand on his rough cheek. "I'm okay."

Damien nodded. "I just ... to think that I almost lost you, again—"

Her slim fingers came up to his lips, effectively silencing him. "Kiss me, Damien," she whispered.

Then her lips were on his, soft and urgent silencing all concerns.

Her kiss was oxygen for a drowning man and, behaving just like one, Damien held on to her for dear life. Their breaths mingled, and he knew then that he'd never be the same person again. Tess was part of him now, and he needed her to know how much she meant to him.

161

Tears rolled down her cheeks. Damien kissed the salty warmth away reverently.

Then her hand came between them, looking for his cock. It was awkward—sex in a bathtub was something that Damien had never attempted before, probably for good reason—and he suddenly worried the bandages on her arm and shoulder were going to end up soaked.

He stood up, lifting her easily in his arms, bringing them both out of the tub.

Her mouth still on his, she came up for air long enough to voice a complaint. "It's cold out here."

He laughed, setting her down on her feet long enough to grab a large bath towel from the rack and enveloping her inside. Then he picked her up again, heading towards the bed.

"You're not going to dry yourself?" she asked.

"In a second," he replied, laying her body on the mattress gently, mindful of her injuries. "You look like a butterfly, about to emerge from its cocoon."

"Like a moth, you mean?" she asked, but she was smiling.

Her nipples were puckered, whether from cold or excitement—or both—he couldn't be sure. He patted her dry, then used the same towel to dry himself quickly.

Her legs opened up of their own accord as his hand found her pussy. She was already wet, and he felt his cock grow hard just from knowing he was the one making her feel this way.

Damien wanted to take it slowly. He wanted to cherish her body and make her understand how important she was to him—but her hips were coming off the bed, looking to get more of the digit he pressed inside her, making him feel out of control.

"I want more," she said, impatiently.

"Another finger?" he teased.

She shook her head. Her green eyes were blazing. "Your cock."

And then he was inside her. The pleasure was so strong, he thought he might come then and there. He inhaled and exhaled roughly a few times, praying for control. Then Tess's core pulsed around him, and he forgot everything.

Mindful to keep his weight off her upper body and to stay away from her injury, he pounded into her. Tess matched each thrust, her legs wrapped around his hips and ass.

"God, Tess ..."

"More, Damien, more," she begged.

Damien's pleasure climbed higher and higher. He was going to come soon, and he wanted—no, needed—to bring her with him.

He looked at Tess. Her eyes were on his cock as it drove in and out of her tight sheath. His hand snaked between their bodies slowly, letting her see what he was doing. His thumb found her.

"Oh God, Damien!"

He strummed her clit gently in time with his relentless pounding—riding the climax higher and higher. Just as Damien thought he couldn't hold on any longer, he heard those magic words from her.

"I'm coming," she moaned.

Her words, and the ensuing clenching of her sex around his cock, were the key to his orgasm. He thrust one more time and emptied himself inside her—the feeling so strong, for a second he wondered if he'd forgotten to sheath himself. He felt with his hand and reassured himself that the condom was in place. He'd never had sex without a condom before—not with Jamie's mother, and not with any other woman—but he couldn't imagine anything sexier than bareback sex with Tess. And the idea of making a baby with her …

This isn't sex, this is love.

Tess's face relaxed into a dreamy contentment. He felt an inordinate amount of pride that he'd been the one to put that look on her face.

"I'm never moving again," she stated, immediately shifting her arms to pull him into a tight embrace.

Damien laughed. "Never again, huh."

Tess smiled and kissed his mouth, his chin, his neck. Her mouth was smooth where he knew his own skin was rough. He tried to move his face away so as not to rough her up with his stubble, but she wasn't having any of it.

"I love you, Tess," he whispered roughly against her ear. The words, so unfamiliar, also felt somehow right.

He felt her tense, was about to reassure her that he didn't expect her to reply in kind, when she brought her own mouth closer to his ear.

"I love you too, Damien," she whispered.

Chapter 17

Tess

Tess woke up from her nap feeling like she could easily sleep twelve hours more. But she knew John was going to be bringing Jamie home for dinner, and she didn't want the boy to worry about her, so she got up.

She stretched her arm gingerly—maybe she would take one of those painkillers the medic had provided. A different part of her anatomy was experiencing a much more pleasurable kind of burn.

Tess blushed as she thought of how hard she'd come, then blushed again as she thought of the aftermath. Damien had told her he loved her. And she'd said the words back.

It wasn't just post-orgasmic bliss—at least not for her. She'd known she loved him for a long time, and the thought that he now knew didn't scare her much.

She wondered how he felt about it.

Is he sorry he said the words?

Tess put on clean underwear and walked to her closet, looking for something to wear. She needed something that wouldn't chafe against the road rash, but that would still keep her bandage covered.

She settled on a light-blue summer dress with ruched sleeves that just reached her elbows. Her beige espadrilles made her feel too dressed up, so she settled for bright orange flip-flops instead.

She walked out of her small studio and towards the main house, entering through the open patio sliding door.

Damien smiled at her from behind the kitchen aisle, where he was busy putting something in the oven. His eyes caressed her from head to foot.

"How are you feeling?" he asked, his voice a deep baritone that reverberated down her spine.

"Much better after that nap," she said.

"And your arm?"

She resisted the urge to roll the shoulder. "It's okay. I might take one of those painkillers?"

He was beside her in an instant, holding out a glass of water and a pill. She took the pill from him, thanking him, and choked it down with a small sip of water.

Damien went back to the kitchen area. "I'm making stir-fried rice," he said. "And peach cobbler for dessert."

One could get used to this kind of food.

Tess realized she was starving. She loved Damien's stir-fried rice, cooked with copious amounts of soy sauce.

Something pinged, and Damien's eyes went to the laptop open on the counter beside him.

"Shit," he breathed. "I'm sorry. We still haven't been able to identify the car," he explained.

Tess understood from his expression that it was a bit like finding a needle in a haystack.

The doorbell rang.

166

"There's Jamie," she said, going to the door. The boy ran inside and hugged Tess tightly.

"Tess!"

"Easy, buddy," Damien said, unwrapping the boy's arms from around her waist.

"Are you okay, Tess?" John asked. His deep, wrinkled eyes were full of concern.

"I'm okay," she said, smiling.

"I'll see you tomorrow, Jamie," John said.

"We're having dinner soon, Dad. Why don't you eat with us?"

"I would, but I'm meeting Sebastian and Kris for dinner tonight."

Tess smiled. *Dinner* seemed to be code for *poker* in John's world—she doubted the men were planning on eating much.

Damien stepped out of the house. "Stay inside and lock the doors. I'll be back in a minute, I'm going to speak with Gael and Kat."

A couple minutes later, Gael and Kat left for the night. A patrol car would drive by later on that night to make sure everything was okay.

"Wash your hands, Jamie, and come back to set the table, please," Damien asked. Jamie ran off towards the bathroom.

"How can I help?" she asked.

Damien moved the stool next to him with his foot. "Sit down and rest, Tess. We'll take care of it today."

He handed her a glass of flavored sparkling water. It was her favorite flavor, and her eyes filled with tears to realize he'd noticed.

"Hey, what's going on?" Damien's concerned expression made her cry even harder. She wiped the tears quickly, looking in the direction Jamie had disappeared in, taking in two deep breaths until she felt slightly more in control.

"I'm okay," she said.

Just then, Jamie came running into the combined kitchen and living room area.

"Are your hands clean?" Damien asked.

Jamie raised them high in the air, as if Damien had a cleanliness meter.

"Spotless," Damien confirmed. "Grab the placemats, please, Jamie."

Jamie set three placemats on the dining table, then went to the drawer to pick up napkins and cutlery. The plates were too high for him to reach, so Tess got off the stool and handed them to him, along with three glasses, which she gave to the boy one at a time. Finally, the boy admired the table. Tess could see him counting carefully to make sure he hadn't missed anything.

"Great job, pumpkin," she said, ruffling the boy's hair affectionately.

"Can I try some?" Jamie asked, clambering onto the stool next to hers and reaching for her glass.

Tess nodded.

"Mmmm," the boy said, licking his lips.

"Hey son," Damien began. His voice was light, but there was an undertone Tess didn't recognize, that made her look up at him. Damien didn't look at her. He was stirring vegetables in the wok, but his gaze was focused on Jamie. "Is it okay with you if I ask Tess to sleep in the house with us?"

What are you doing, Damien?

Jamie looked up at his dad. "Is she scared because of the car?" he asked. Tess wondered where he'd heard about the incident. Probably overheard John, Gael and Kat talking about it.

Perceptive kid.

"No. She's not scared—there's nothing to be scared about, but I'll sleep better knowing she's close to us."

Jamie nodded, his expression serious.

"So we can take care of her."

"So we can take care of her," Damien confirmed. He then took a deep breath. "It's not just tonight. I would like to ask her to move in with us. What do you think, buddy?"

Tess watched Jamie's expression carefully, and she suddenly realized that's why Damien had waited until she was there before speaking to the boy. He'd wanted her to see the boy's reaction first-hand.

Jamie's face lit up in a big smile. "Of course, daddy. She's family—I know that already."

Tess felt tears roll down her face again.

"Tess?" Jamie asked uncertainly.

"I'm okay, Jamie."

"But you're crying."

"I am, but they're happy tears."

"Oh, okay," the boy said, looking like a carbon copy of his dad. "Where will she sleep, dad?"

Damien's eyes locked with hers, and she couldn't have looked away even if she'd tried. His voice was soft as he replied. "I'd like her to sleep in my room with me, buddy."

Jamie nodded, his expression serious once again. "That makes sense—your bed is bigger than mine."

Damien laughed. "But you know you can still come to our bed anytime."

Our bed.

There was a question in Damien's eyes now, and the answer was a resounding yes. She wanted to jump into his arms and scream to the rooftops, but settled with nodding lightly in response.

"Dinner's ready. Hand me your plates, both of you," Damien said, spooning a generous serving of rice onto the first plate.

Chapter 18

Damien

After Jamie was asleep, Damien and Tess had made love once again. This time, their love-making had been gentle, and they'd fallen asleep in each other's arms.

In the morning, he'd helped her move some of her things to his room—their room, now. She'd still be using the studio to write, but at night they'd sleep together.

Today was a Saturday, so Jamie didn't have summer camp. That made it easier for Damien to ask him and Tess to please stay home. They still hadn't been able to trace the Porsche, and Damien didn't want them going anywhere until they had a better idea who tried to hurt Tess.

Damien's father had volunteered to come spend the day—he and Jamie were going to build a dog house in the yard. Damien wasn't about to ask who the dog house was for—he'd cross that bridge when he got to it.

Tess promised Damien she'd stay home, claiming she wanted to catch up on her writing. He wasn't sure whether she was still scared or just wanted to reassure him.

As soon as he arrived in the office, Jens and Drake followed him inside. Both men looked like they hadn't slept much, and Damien felt a moment of guilt.

"Any luck?" he asked, while he took off his jacket. He already knew from the men's frowns what the answer was.

"We have a list of over eighty cars to go through still." Drake cleared his throat. "But something arrived fifteen minutes ago—a letter."

Damien stopped what he was doing and stared back at the men. "A letter?"

"Addressed to you, *Commandant*. It came inside a bigger box, and the letter itself was wrapped around a large rock. The mailroom team opened it and took it to the lab, but I have a copy here for you."

Damien grabbed the photocopy. A large, almost childish scrawl stared back at him.

Five years ago, you ruined my life. Now I'm going to do the same to you. Nobody you love will ever be safe.

He flipped the paper around, forgetting it was a copy.

"There was nothing else, Damien, just those three sentences," Drake confirmed, his expression guarded.

Damien sat at his desk, still holding the paper in his hand. His heart sped up as he reread the threat. He'd gotten threats before—not many, but a few. None of them ended up meaning anything. But this one felt different. It was too much of a coincidence, coming so soon after Tess's accident—the two things had to be related.

"Yesterday we thought maybe that Russian billionaire was holding a grudge, but he got on a plane shortly after— claims he'll never return to France, and is in fact thinking of suing the French government for false advertising," Drake said. "And now, with the mention of something that happened five years ago …"

"Get Isolde Durant here, please."

172

With a sharp nod that reminded Damien of his friend's military background, Drake left the office. Jens stood there, looking at him sympathetically.

"The threat is growing. I'm calling in the team. We'll meet in the conference room in an hour, but I'd like you to do me a favor. Go to my place and stay with Tess and Jamie today."

Jens nodded, flexing his large muscles. "I'll be their shadow, *Commandant*."

Damien called Tess to let her know Jens was on his way and reiterate the warning for them to stay home. He was hanging up when he saw Drake escorting a curvy young woman towards his office.

That was quick.

It shouldn't have surprised him—Isolde Durant's office was on the top floor of the building. Damien had been there before—the windows were large, with a superb view of Mont Blanc. Apparently the view encouraged Dr. Durant's patients to open up to her.

"*Commandant*," she said respectfully.

"Thanks for coming, Dr. Durant."

"Isolde, please," she said quickly.

"Please sit, Isolde. Did Drake update you as to what happened?"

"Only the basics, but I'd like to hear the rest from you," she said, looking behind her to see where Drake had settled. The man stood by the window, his back ramrod straight—Damien remembered now what he'd forgotten before, that Drake and Isolde had met before, and were not on the best of terms.

Over the next three minutes, Damien updated the police psychologist on everything that had happened to date.

She sat with her hands primly clasped in front of her, listening intently. Finally, she spoke. Her voice had a soothing tone to it.

"With all due respect, *Commandant*, I'm not sure how much help I'll be. I'm a police psychologist—not a criminal profiler." Her hands shifted inwards until she was pointing at herself. Damien's gaze followed to take in her black pants, paired with a tunic-like pale blue shirt and black suit jacket that did nothing to disguise her generous curves. On her feet, she wore a pair of professional-looking black leather pumps.

Damien looked into her honey-colored eyes. "I know that. We'll try to get a profiler from Annecy in as soon as possible." He lowered his voice. "What I'm asking for here is a personal favor. I'd like to hear your opinion about this letter—my team and I need all the help we can get. Please, Isolde."

"Okay," she acceded. With her foot she pushed out the other visitor's chair towards Drake, who took the hint and sat down as well. "I agree with you that it's too much of a coincidence, coming right after the incident you just told me about. Whoever wrote this letter was angry."

"How do you know that?" Damien asked. "Is it the scrawl?"

"I'm not a graphologist," she said, shaking her head. Her brown curls bobbed up and down. "He blames you, specifically, for something that happened five years ago—something that ruined their life. Without knowing what that was, it's hard to—"

Damien nodded. "Drake, I've asked the team to gather for a conference call in just under forty minutes. Ask them to find all files that match that period, please."

Drake nodded tightly and left the room.

"What else?"

"It's very personal. But you know that already. Not just because the letter came addressed to you, but because of the words themselves."

Isolde re-read the letter with emphasis on certain words. "Five years ago *you* ruined my life. Now I'm going to do the same to *you*. Nobody *you* love will ever be safe."

Damien raked his fingers through his hair. "I need to find this person, Isolde. I have a son—and a woman who means more to me than my own life. I can't let them get hurt. What would you do in my shoes?"

"Here's what I would do, Damien, and again, this is my personal recommendation—I'm not equipped to give you a professional opinion. I'd go through all the cases from between four and six years ago, to allow for people's skewered perception of time. It has to be a case that you were personally involved in. The writer uses the word *ruined*, so I'd look for cases where somebody died, or was very seriously injured—a child, an adult … it could even be a pet."

Damien nodded. Everything she was saying made sense.

"And I would keep your girlfriend and son under constant watch, Damien. I don't need to tell you how unbalanced this individual sounds."

"Thanks for your help, Isolde."

She stood up and straightened her clothes. "Let me know if I can help with anything else."

#

Damien looked around the conference room, where Drake, Kat, Gael and Hiro sat, poring through case documents.

On the center of the large table stood three piles—a large, teetering pile of files they still had to go through, and two smaller piles, one with the cases that didn't match what they were looking for, either because nobody had been hurt or because he hadn't been personally involved, and a second one with files that warranted a closer look.

Other teams had offered to support them, but Damien thought it better to limit it to his team alone for now—while Kat and Gael hadn't been part of the team five years earlier, they were all used to Search and Rescue work. They knew, where other teams might not, the types of cases they were called out on, and which ones posed greater or lesser risk.

Damien dropped the file he was looking at into the *not-to-worry-about* pile and paced the conference room. Five years ago he'd been a lieutenant, working alongside Drake, Jens, and several other colleagues who'd since left the department or become PGHM trainers, like their old commander. He looked at Bailey, lying so quietly at Hiro's feet. Five years ago she hadn't even been born yet.

Damien clenched his hands into fists. This was like looking for a needle in a haystack. The Chamonix PGHM responded to over twelve hundred calls a year. His team alone responded to over four hundred calls.

"*Commandant*?" a voice asked. Damien looked up to see Colonel Pelegrin sticking his gray head through the door. Damien walked outside to meet his boss. "Colonel," he said formally.

"Do you need anything, Damien?" the older man said. Damien was reminded again of how lucky he was to work with the people he worked with.

"We're still going through the files. I'll let you know what we come up with, Colonel."

"And somebody is with your son?"

"Jens Melkopf is with him," Damien said. He'd been in touch with Jens regularly since the man had arrived at his home. Damien wasn't taking any chances.

"Good, good. Anything we can do to support, let us know. Please focus on this. The other two teams know what's going on, they'll run any rescues themselves until further notice."

"Thank you, Sir," Damien said. He walked back into the conference room, where Kat was now pacing the room, looking pale.

"Kat?" Damien asked worriedly. "Are you okay?"

"I'm sorry," she said, raising her eyes to meet his. "It's just—hard, thinking about all the times we lost someone. You try to put it aside, in your day-to-day, but to see them now, all the people we failed—"

Damien grasped the younger woman's arm. "Hey. We save hundreds of people each year. It's hard to lose some, but think of the people who wouldn't be here if it wasn't for us," he said, pointing to the pile of successful rescues.

An instant later, Bailey was up as well, licking Kat's free hand. The dog was perceptive. Kat smiled and ruffled Bailey's hair affectionately.

"I'll keep going. I just need a minute first—" she said, extricating herself from his hold gently.

"Take your time, Kat," Damien said.

From across the room, he caught Drake's eye. The man's jaw was clenched tight.

"What do you have, Drake?"

"Nothing, so far. There are too many cases. We need to narrow it down."

Five hours later, the pile of cases to look at in more detail had grown substantially larger.

Kat tugged on her ponytail. "These are all the cases involving women or children," she said, swallowing hard. "In all cases there was a husband or father left behind."

Damien rubbed his hair. He needed to get home to Jamie and Tess, but didn't want to leave it like this, with no hope for resolution. Suddenly, he had an idea. "How many of these rescues involved local victims?"

"Local victims?" Hiro asked. At his feet, Bailey snoozed.

"The car had a local license plate. The kidnapper could have rented it or stolen it, but let's work on the assumption that it's his. That means he's from here—in which case we could ignore all rescues involving visitors and tourists."

Hiro picked up the pile and sat down on the floor. Bailey's eyes followed him for a moment, then closed again. "Okay. It's worth a shot." He opened one file after another, this time focusing only on the victim's address. He went through the pile mechanically, and after ten minutes had narrowed it down to nine cases.

"It might be one of these. All local cases—in all cases the victims were women or children." He swallowed hard. "In all cases, there was at least one person we didn't save."

"Take me through them, Hiro, please." Damien looked around the room at Kat, Gael and Drake. "Maybe you should go take a walk."

"We're not going anywhere, Damien," Drake growled. They all moved closer.

Hiro straightened his back against the wall. He picked up the first file carefully and respectfully in both hands. "June five years ago," he began. "There was a fire in a campsite. Another camper called for help on his mobile phone, but by the time the firefighters arrived, the tent was destroyed. A mother and her two young sons died."

"I remember that night," Damien said. His hands clenched into a tight fist. "There wasn't much we could do except keep onlookers away and wait for the doctor to certify the death."

"Was the father there?" Kat asked.

"I don't remember a father."

Hiro leafed through the rest of the file. "No mention of a father here."

"An entire family died that night …" Damien felt himself waver and held on to the table for support. He always hated losing anyone, but ever since he'd become a father, the thought of a child dying affected him more than he could say.

"We need to find out if there's a father, and where he lives now," Damien said.

Hiro set the file down carefully on the floor next to him and picked up the next one. "A helicopter crash. A family of four killed, along with the pilot."

Damien shook his head. "We recovered the aircraft, but there was nothing we could do for the people inside. They all died on impact."

"We need to look for something more personal," Gael said, baring his teeth. "A rescue you were involved in, *jefe*."

Hiro nodded and looked to the next file. His Adam's apple bobbed up and down for a moment, and Damien wasn't sure he wanted to hear about this one. "March five years ago—a young boy lost in the mountains. The search went on for days, but the boy was dead by the time we found him."

Damien nodded. He remembered the case well. The helicopter had found a jacket but it wasn't the right color, so they'd ignored it in the first passes. It was only later that they'd gone back, and realized the jacket was inside out—it was the orange lining that they were seeing from the helicopter. They began to search that area in earnest, but by then it was too late.

Damien steeled himself against the onslaught of guilt. They'd all suffered from it. Even now, years later, it was easy to go back to that moment in time, and feel the pain anew. They'd all been exhausted—and to find the child, dead from exposure, had been one of the single worst moments of his life. One that had threatened to break him, as well as other members of the team.

"We need to speak to his parents," he said, making a note.

"I'm sorry. I need to stretch my legs before we continue," Kat said, walking out of the room. They all chose to ignore the fact that her eyes were full of tears.

"We all need a break," Gael said. He offered Hiro his palm and helped the other man stand.

"I'll get an officer to check up on these families," Hiro said, holding on to the files they'd singled out.

"Make sure Dr. Durant gets a copy of these as well, please. I'd like to get her opinion."

"I'll go ask her now," Drake said, nodding tightly. Then, in a lower voice, he added, "We're going to find him, Damien."

Damien nodded. There was no other choice—he needed to find this man in order to keep his family safe.

Chapter 19

Tess

Two hundred and forty eight.

That was the sum total of words Tess had written, after spending all day at her desk.

At this rate, I'll finish the novel sometime in the next decade.

She gave up in the early afternoon and went to find Jamie and John in the main house.

Coming in through the sliding door, she started as she saw a large man by the kitchen sink—then relaxed when she saw it was Jens, Damien's colleague. The glass he was holding looked small in his huge hands.

She didn't know the man well, beyond the fact that he was the team's doctor as well as a rescue specialist.

"Hi Jens," she said, hating the way her voice shook.

He nodded in her direction, his large body relaxed against the kitchen counter. Jens's face was made up of strong, elegant lines, from his aquiline nose to his strong jaw, but his brown eyes were warm and kind—he seemed to understand that his presence here was a reminder that she wasn't safe.

I'm afraid.

The admission was accompanied by relief. She'd fought against it all night and all morning—trying to write as if nothing were going on—but maybe it was okay for her to be afraid, for her to find herself unable to string two words together or even think about work. Somebody had tried to kill her.

Tess went over to the sink and stood beside him, filling her own glass of water. One thing she loved about living in Chamonix was how the water from the tap was always cold and fresh, regardless of the time of year. She drank a couple tentative sips—then, when her stomach didn't clench, downed the glass.

She felt Jens watching her.

"How are you holding up? Would you like me to change the bandages on your arm?" he asked.

So he's also heard about what happened.

"Damien changed them for me this morning. It was looking okay. But thank you."

He nodded.

"I can't go outside, right?" she asked him.

Jens shook his head apologetically. "Sorry, not unless somebody goes with you, and I can't be in two places at the same time."

"I understand. It's okay."

Except it wasn't. It wasn't something Tess could explain—she was a writer, she'd gone days without leaving her room in the past. But in recent months she'd made a point of going out for a hike, a swim or a run every morning, and not being able to leave the house felt—constricting.

"We can talk to Damien when he's back. He called a few minutes ago to say he was leaving the office. He should be here soon."

She nodded.

"You must be looking forward to that. No more babysitting."

Jens frowned. "Keeping you and Jamie safe is not babysitting."

Why did I say that?

"I'm sorry," she said lamely. "I don't know why I said that."

Jens's frown cleared up, and he nodded. "It's okay."

Before she could embarrass herself further, she moved towards the boy and his grandfather, who were both on the floor, surrounded by Lego pieces of all shapes and colors.

Jamie was wearing a look of intense concentration, as was the case when he was immersed in a Lego construction. He didn't even notice she was there.

When Tess had first arrived in Chamonix, she'd spent hours googling the best organizational methods for the little pieces, looking for a system that would keep the pieces off the floor but allow Jamie to find them whenever he needed them.

Nothing had worked. Jamie liked them best in a large bucket that he could overturn when he started playing. It always amazed her, the complex creations Jamie was able to put together, at only five years old.

She'd watched his process, whereby he'd spend a few seconds, up to a minute, searching for the perfect piece. She understood now that time wasn't time wasted—while he looked for the piece, his mind was thinking ahead to the rest of the construction. It was exactly like when she sat down to write—she had a vague idea of where she was going, but the details she only fleshed out once she was inside the book.

185

So she'd given up on fixing Jamie's system—it wasn't broken in the first place, and the Lego pieces were easy enough to place back in their large buckets when he was done playing.

"Hi Jamie, hi John" she said. They both looked up from the Lego.

John winked at her. "You're going to have to help me get up," he said in his raspy voice.

"Sure. Just let me know when you want to get up, John," Tess said, laughing.

The older man looked at her for a moment too long—it seemed to Tess that he was also checking up on her, trying to determine if she was okay. Tess liked Damien's father—she knew he and Damien had a complicated relationship, but John had always treated her kindly and it was clear he doted on Jamie.

Lately, however, she'd started feeling uncomfortable around the older man—like she was keeping a secret from him.

Since I started sleeping with his son.

It had nothing to do with John, of course, and everything to do with her, and the uncertainty in her and Damien's relationship.

Damien asked me to move in.

He sort of told his son about us.

Does that mean I'm Damien's girlfriend now?

It was a conversation she and Damien would have to have together at some point, but it seemed foolish to think of such things when there was somebody out there trying to kill them.

"I'll help as well, grandpa," Jamie said, his expression serious. "But first, look at the chameleon's tail. It has a light, so he can see where he's going."

Tess heard a car and moved towards the window.

"Stay away from the window, please, Tess," Jens asked tersely. She hadn't even heard him move, yet suddenly he was standing beside her. "It's okay. It's Damien—he's home."

Chapter 20

Damien

As soon as he set eyes on Tess Damien knew, from the tight expression on her face, that she wasn't doing well.

Physically, he didn't have any concerns. Tess's injuries from the previous day were mild and seemed to be healing well, and Jens had told him everything had been quiet all day.

Damien trusted Jens with his life. Of the entire team, Jens was perhaps the most overqualified—a doctor, he'd been a member of the German Special Forces Command for ten years before joining the PGHM. He knew that anybody trying to hurt Jamie and Tess while Jens was with them would pay for it dearly—just like he knew that, if necessary, Jens would lay down his life to protect them.

Emotionally, however, Damien could tell Tess was worn out—and, from the way she glanced at the doorway every so often, that she really needed to get out of the house.

Before his father left for the night, Damien asked him if he could stay home with Jamie the next morning, knowing the older man would say yes. Jens had immediately offered to come back as well, even though it was a Saturday and he was meant to be off.

Damien himself had spent half the night poring over more old case files, looking to see if any other cases jogged his memory.

He'd never seen Tess smile as widely as when he'd told her they had the entire morning to themselves.

"This is incredible, Damien," she said, staring at the walls of the Mer de Glace ice cave. They were the only ones in the cave—they'd taken the first train up, since he knew it'd get packed later on in the day. "I'd read about it but didn't imagine it could be this serene up here," she admitted.

Although Damien had been to the cave multiple times, he saw it now through her eyes—the thick layers of ice, so dense it looked blue, the heavy silence of the glacier. Even the tacky ice sculptures depicting animals and objects, which were redone every year, seemed almost endearing to him this time around.

As corny as it sounded, and it wasn't something he was planning to say out loud, Tess was by far the most beautiful thing in the cave.

"Coming up here is the first thing most visitors do when they arrive in Chamonix, yet half the people living in town have never been here," he shared, smiling.

"I'll have to tell them about it when we get back," she said, pulling her woolen hat over her ears. "Brrr ... it really *is* cold here. I thought you were crazy when you suggested I bring a hat and gloves, but I'm glad I listened."

Shortly after, they left the cave and started walking back up the stairs that would take them back up to the cable car station.

He held her gloved hand to his face, kissing it gently and blowing his hot breath on her fingers. Her body melted against him in a warm embrace.

"Hey, keep that for later, or I won't be able to climb all these steps," she said. "Let's see if I can beat you to the top!"

She climbed the stairs three at a time. He stopped for a moment, enjoying the view, as her short coat and black leggings did nothing to hide her ass. Together, they passed the step marking the level the glacier used to start in 1990, then kept going up. They were almost at the top of the stairs when Damien's phone rang. It was Drake's number.

"Gray," he said.

"Just wanted to share a quick update, Damien, regarding the files we set aside yesterday. Three of the families moved away from the area after the incident—they say they haven't been back since. We're checking with local police, but so far they seem to be telling the truth."

Damien nodded. "What about the others?"

"The officer caught up with one family in the hospital, where the mother just gave birth to a baby boy."

"So it's not them."

"We're still trying to reach the remaining two, as well as the files you shared last night. It doesn't look like you got much sleep, boss."

Damien couldn't disagree. He was exhausted. For a moment his attention wandered. He forced himself to focus on what Drake was saying.

"… appointment with Dr. Durant in an hour to look through them together."

"Thank you, Drake. I'll come into the office after lunch."

"We'll catch up then, Damien."

Damien disconnected the call. He turned around to find Tess looking at him wearily.

"Is everything okay?"

Damien shook his head. "No news for now. But we're going to figure this out, Tess."

She nodded. "I believe that, Damien. I really do. It's just … I've never felt like this before. I feel like I've got the sword of Damocles hanging over my head—over Jamie's head. Could we maybe go back home, please?" she asked, shivering.

Damien nodded. "We can catch the train and be home in—"

In his pocket, the phone rang again. He picked it up, thinking Drake had forgotten something, but heard his father's voice on the phone instead.

"Damien?" His father sounded out of breath and hesitant. Damien's stomach lurched—John was never, ever hesitant.

"Dad? What happened? Is Jamie okay?"

"Jamie's gone," John said, his voice breaking in a sob. "There was a motorcycle outside … a man … he threw something through the window. The room filled with gas …. that's the last thing I remember. When I woke up Jamie wasn't there."

Damien held on to the handrail for dear life. His fear became a living, palpable thing inside him.

Not again.

Please, not again.

Damien knew he needed to hold it together, that Jamie's very life depended on them making the right decisions now.

"Dad, put Jens on the phone."

192

"He's … still unconscious," his father said, his voice heavy. "He has a pulse, but he was closer to the window. I need to get him outside …"

"I'll get help, Dad. Leave the line open."

Damien looked back at Tess. Her face was chalky, the freckles on the bridge of her nose standing out like beacons on her face. She'd clearly heard enough of the conversation.

"Oh God," she squeaked. "Jamie's been taken?"

Damien nodded grimly.

Tess's hand went to her mouth. She looked exactly like he felt, like she might need to throw up.

"He's gone because we weren't there," she whispered.

Jamie's gone because I wasn't there to protect him.

Intellectually, Damien knew neither statement was true. If Jens hadn't been able to do anything, neither he nor Tess could have done anything either. He knew that. And yet, the sense of having failed his son was strong and bitter in his mouth. The guilt lay entirely with him, not with Tess.

Damien slammed his hand onto the handrail. The sharp pain helped to clear his head.

Start thinking, Damien. Start thinking.

"We don't know how long my father was unconscious. We need to call Drake."

Tess nodded. In her eyes Damien could see the unshed tears she was working so hard to keep inside, but he couldn't comfort her now. If he did, he'd break—and then Jamie would be lost to him forever. He turned towards the glacier, bringing out his phone again.

#

Tess

Tess bit her lip to keep from crying out loud. Damien didn't need her distracting him—but dammit, it hurt when he turned away.

This is my fault.

Damien came up here today because of me, and now Jamie's gone.

It's my fault.

Another voice inside her tried to shush the first voice, telling her this wasn't on her head, that the kidnapper was to blame.

Jamie must be so scared.

At least last time I was there with him.

Tess put her hand over her mouth to stop herself from sobbing.

Damien's free hand was white where it clenched the handrail.

She heard him speak with Drake for a second, but the roaring in her ears made it hard to listen to his words. He was sending someone to check on Jens and his father, she understood that.

Jamie's gone.

What if this time he's gone forever?

Suddenly, Damien exclaimed. "I have an incoming call from an unknown number, Drake. I'm putting you on hold." Then a second later, he spoke again, his voice hard. "Gray."

"Damien Gray. Finally, we get to speak."

Tess was standing close enough that she could hear the deep voice on the other end of the phone—as clearly as she had weeks earlier, when the man had stopped her by the waterfall and asked her the time, except that time he'd spoken in English with her.

Though they were standing still, Tess felt as if the ground were dissolving around her. "That voice. It's the same man," she whispered, holding on to Damien's sleeve.

Damien's voice went hard. "Who are you? Where's my son?"

"Let's not worry about the first question for now. You already know I have your son."

"Is Jamie okay?" Damien asked, anguish breaking his voice. "Let me speak with him, please."

"The boy is fine. Now listen to me, you're going to go to the Aiguille du Midi."

The tightness around Damien's mouth grew. "It will take me hours to get there," he lied.

The man roared. For a second, Tess was sure he was going to hang up. Then his words came again. "Lie to me again, Gray, and the next time you hear from Jamie will be when you get a piece of him in the mail."

"Please don't hurt him," Damien begged.

"I know you and the woman are up in the mountains. Bring her to me now, and I'll let you choose which one of them lives. You have two hours."

"I need more time."

"Two hours, Gray. Just you and the woman. If I see so much as a lost hiker in the area, your son dies."

"Please ..." Damien began. "Fuck. He hung up."

Tess felt herself begin to shake. She forced herself to uncurl her fingers from where they were digging into Damien's arm. The last thing Damien needed was to have to worry about her. But the shaking got worse, and suddenly

195

there wasn't enough air in the mountains to breathe. She suddenly realized she was in the middle of a full-blown panic attack.

"Breathe, Tess, breathe," Damien said roughly against her ear. He sounded worried. Then he was pulling her into his arms and down onto the floor, pushing her head forward between her legs.

As soon as she started breathing again, her head cleared. "We need to go," she said, pulling against his arm. She'd seen the signs to Aiguille du Midi, and it was a long hike.

"Stay down, Tess, breathe," Damien said, his voice gentler now. Then he was on the phone with someone again.

"I need your help. I got a call from the kidnapper. He's got Jamie—wants me to head to Aiguille du Midi and hand Tess over as well."

The conversation went on for a couple more minutes, but Tess wasn't able to hear the voice on the other side. Then Damien kneeled down next to her.

"Tess? Honey? Are you okay?"

Her eyes filled with tears at his gentle tone. She looked up into his penetrating blue eyes. They were still full of worry, but something else shone in them as well now, something that looked like hope.

"Tess, listen to me. The man is waiting for something—he'll keep Jamie alive until then. We're going to get him back."

She nodded, wanting to believe him but struggling to wrap her head around what was happening.

"So what do we do?"

"Kat and Drake were at the station already. They'll take a helo and come here to pick us up. Kat will drop us off at the Aiguille du Midi and then take you back—"

"What?"

Damien repeated himself patiently, his eyes taking on a worried look. "I said Kat will take you into town and—"

"No," Tess said.

"Yes," Damien replied with finality.

Tess shook her head. She was feeling stronger now. "He said I have to be there."

The madman's words resonated in her mind.

He's going to make Damien choose.

Damien breathed out. "We can't take orders from a madman. And I couldn't bear it if something happened to you, Tess," he said.

"He said to bring me along," Tess repeated stonily. "You and your team do whatever you have to do, but I have to be there. We're not going to risk Jamie's life."

"I don't like it."

"You don't have to like it. We don't have a choice, Damien."

He considered her words carefully for a moment. She saw the slight shake of his head that told her she'd won.

"What about your dad and Jens?"

"Gael is already on his way, with an ambulance. They'll take care of them and look for any clues." Damien took her hand in his. "Come on, we need to get to a spot where the helicopter can pick us up."

Chapter 21

Damien

Whenever he worked a rescue with a rookie, Damien always made sure the young man or woman had something to do—it was the best way to keep panic at bay.

Damien used that trick on himself now. He could keep it together, so long as he had something to do—but, like a shark, if he stopped swimming for a moment, he felt he might lose it. And he had to stay strong. Search and Rescue wasn't always about immediate results. Sometimes it was about staying power, about keeping the faith when the odds looked insurmountable.

He looked out of the helicopter window at the mountains beneath them, then back towards Tess, who sat in front of him, her hat held in her hands. She looked pale but in control. He knew he should reach over and comfort her, but his body and brain were numb—he couldn't move.

Drake walked back towards them from the co-pilot seat.

"Kat's going to patch Hiro in," he said. "He thinks he's got something."

Damien nodded and picked up the headset by his knees, putting it on. He watched Tess do the same, her look almost defiant as she looked in his direction.

"What did you find, Hiro?"

"I went back to the original case files, looking for someone who might fit the description of the man Jens saw outside your house this morning."

Damien forced himself to keep silent, waiting for Hiro to go on.

"I focused on incidents near where you are—and I think I found something. There was an accident almost five years ago, near Aiguille du Midi."

That wasn't strange. Aiguille du Midi was a common accident site for mountaineers and skiers. The PGHM got called out there several times every season.

"What happened?"

"A man and his son were climbing the north face of the Aiguille du Midi. The boy was too young, the climb too technical. They were both exhausted but hanging on when they called for help, but by the time we arrived, the boy had fallen to his death."

"Why didn't we flag this case file first time around?"

"The victim had just turned eighteen—he wasn't technically a child anymore."

And just like that, Damien knew exactly what case they were speaking about.

Damien had already been in the area at the time, so he'd been the first person to arrive on site, before his commander or any of the other team members. He'd also been the one to tell his father his son was dead.

The boy had fallen eight hundred meters down the ridge to his death—all he'd been able to do was certify his death. Damien recalled the boy's broken body—such a waste, he remembered thinking.

An image of the father flashed in his mind—a large, wooden-looking man, overcome by the horror of the situation. He'd tried to punch Damien, screaming that they could have saved his son if they'd gotten there faster. Damien had held the man until the medic could administer a shot.

They'd both been evacuated in the same helicopter—the father unconscious, the son dead.

"The father's name is Roger Dubois," Hiro added. "He's a farmer, owns significant acreage."

"This was five years ago?" That was Kat's voice on the headset, from the pilot seat.

"Yes—must have been shortly before you joined us. We didn't even have our own pilot at the time, we shared one with the Annecy unit."

"What I don't understand," Damien continued, "is why now? It's been five years. I need you to go to the Dubois home now, Hiro. See what you can figure out, and call us."

"But, Damien, we should get the team together and come find you—"

"No. Jamie's life depends on us doing as the man asked, and he asked that we go alone. We're already risking much by having Kat and Drake here."

"If you're sure, *Commandant*."

"I'm sure. See what you can find about Roger Dubois and call me back, Hiro."

Drake disconnected the call.

"How far are we, Kat?" Damien asked into the headset.

"I can drop you off on the west face, where you requested, and you walk the rest of the way, or I could get you a bit closer."

"Drop me off. We don't want him to hear the helicopter and get spooked. I'll walk." He looked down at his watch. It was going to be tight, but he could do it.

"What are you talking about? We're going to do this again?" Tess asked, picking up on his pronoun use.

Damien sighed inwardly. He stretched his long legs and took off the headset, pointing to Tess to do the same so they could have a private conversation.

"I still think you should stay in the helicopter," he began.

She nodded. "I've made a mental note of what you think, Damien. But I'm coming with you."

"Kat and I could go—"

"Yeah, because Kat's fiery red hair looks just like mine," she said, looking disgruntled.

Damien took a deep breath.

"I don't want you there, Tess."

Her eyes shone with green fire.

"I don't really care what you want, Damien. We have to get Jamie back, and we're not going to give that asshole any excuse to hurt him."

Damien clenched his hands. He knew what she was saying was true.

"You'll do as I say?"

"I'll do as you say, Damien, as long as I don't think it poses a risk to Jamie's life." Once again, Damien's eyes filled with tears. "I love him too, you know?"

"I know, Tess. I know."

He turned to speak with Drake. "Tess and I will get off and walk to the hut. I want Kat to keep the helo out of sight but stay close."

Drake nodded tightly. "Where do you want me?"

"Do you have your climbing equipment?"

"You know I do, Damien."

"I'd like you to climb up the north face. We'll be wearing our ear pieces, so you'll be able to hear things." It was a big ask—though a competent climber, rock climbing wasn't one of Drake's favorite pastimes.

Drake didn't hesitate. "I can do that."

#

Tess

"Are you sure about this, Tess?" Damien asked. He grabbed on to her hand so hard she thought she might bruise. It was the only outward sign that he wasn't completely in control.

It was ironic that she—who was so out of her element in this world—would have to be the one to reassure Damien, but she knew him well enough by now to know what was going on in his mind.

Damien was a protector—it was in his nature, and it was also his job, what he'd trained his whole life for. He wouldn't hesitate to lay down his life for her or Jamie—but that wasn't what was being required of him now.

Tess fought to steady her breathing. Though Damien looked like he was merely out for an early afternoon stroll, the hike to the abandoned hut had taken a toll on her.

"I trust you, Damien. I know you'll do everything you can to get us home safely, and I wouldn't want any other man by my side," she said carefully. If things didn't go according to plan, she didn't want to say anything that would make it harder for him to move on.

His nostrils flared on a sharp inhale. He was about to say something else when his phone rang again.

Upon hearing the man's voice on the other end of the phone, her knees started shaking. The expression "quaking knees" was one she'd used before in her writing, but not one she'd ever experienced in real life. Her hands, too, were shaking—she pressed them roughly against her thighs. If Damien learned the true extent of her fear, he'd never let her go on with it.

Tess pressed herself closer to Damien—she needed to hear the other end of the conversation.

"… into the hut. You stay outside."

"She's not going anywhere until we see Jamie," Damien said firmly. "We need to know he's okay."

The man clucked and did something that had Jamie screaming in the background. "Daddy!"

"Stop, don't hurt him—" Damien begged. Tess pressed herself against his hip, steadying him, lending him her strength.

"She has sixty seconds to walk inside, or the boy dies," the man said roughly, disconnecting the call.

"Jamie's inside," Damien said.

"I promise I'll do everything I can to keep him safe, Damien," she whispered.

"I need both of you safe," he said, hugging her to him. His expression was agonized.

And suddenly Tess felt calm. Her knees, which had been trembling seconds before, were still—even her breaths seemed to have settled into her belly.

It was time to take back control of the situation.

"Anything else I need to know?" she asked, surprised by her almost casual tone.

Damien shook his head. He held on to her hand and caressed it gently. "I don't want you carrying any weapons. Just try to keep him talking, and know that I'll come for you."

She wanted to kiss him, to press her lips against his and feel his strength, but she didn't want to risk losing her newfound courage. She turned around and walked towards the hut.

Should I be raising my arms?

Don't want to get shot if I can avoid it.

She lifted her arms away from her body slightly so her hands were both visible.

As she approached the house a rough voice spoke from inside—it was the same man who'd been on the phone with Damien, the same man who'd kidnapped them that day by the waterfall.

"Don't come any closer."

Tess stopped immediately.

"Take off your jacket."

Her fingers shook slightly as she undid the zipper of her jacket and took it off. She'd taken off her jumper earlier in the hike, so she was just wearing a pale blue tank top. She felt naked but resisted the urge to cross her arms over her chest. This wasn't the time to show weakness.

The wooden door groaned and opened a crack to reveal a large heavy-set man. He wasn't wearing a hat this time, so Tess took her time inspecting his face. He was older than she'd originally thought when she'd seen him by the waterfall, probably in his late forties. Still, he looked strong as an ox. His hands were large and square, the nails bitten to stubs.

"Leave that on the ground," he ordered. "Now turn around."

Tess bristled at this last order but turned around slowly. She hadn't realized when she'd gotten dressed that morning what a great outfit choice she'd made—neither the leggings nor the tank top could hide any kind of weapon.

"Come inside," he said roughly.

"I want to see Jamie first," she said, wishing her voice sounded stronger.

She took a quick step back as the door opened fully—she hadn't expected him to do as she said. Peering behind the man, she saw a small shape huddled in the corner.

"Jamie!" Tess shouted, and suddenly she was running into the hut, past the large man, who moved aside quickly for someone his size.

She dove for the corner where Jamie sat, barely even noticing the wooden door closing behind her. Jamie sat with his little knees up against his chest, his expression pinched— he wasn't crying now, but his eyes were red-rimmed, his round blue glasses stained with dried tears.

For a moment Jamie didn't move, as if he couldn't really believe his eyes—then he launched his little body against hers, slamming into her so hard she would have lost her balance if she wasn't already falling to her knees beside him.

"Jamie, are you okay?" she said, struggling to keep herself from crying. She had to stay strong—for both of them.

"Tess!" Jamie sniffled, hiding his face in Tess's chest. She held his trembling body and scowled at the man who'd dared scare Jamie in this way. She wasn't a violent person by nature—all her life she'd been the girl to argue that the pen was mightier than the sword—yet right now she wanted nothing more than to hurt this man.

But she was also a realist. She would not win a fight against him—what she had to do was wait, trust in Damien and his team and, when the time came, be ready to protect Jamie.

"Where's my daddy?"

"It's going to be okay," she said soothingly, not wanting to speak of Damien in the madman's presence. "I'm here with you, and I'm not going anywhere."

Tess raised her eyes to the man, who stood by stolidly. "So," she said, and she didn't even try to hide the contempt in her tone. "What now?"

"Give me your hands," he said laconically. He produced a rope from his pocket, which he tied around Tess's wrists in a practiced move. She swallowed a wave of revulsion as his calloused fingers touched her skin, but didn't make any move to stop him.

At least he's not tying them behind my back.

The man muttered something to himself that she couldn't make out. He held on to the free end of the rope, tugging on her wrists—hard enough that Tess had to move to avoid losing her balance. "Outside. Now."

"You are a bad man!" Jamie shouted, baring his little teeth at the man. He seemed ready to fight, and Tess had never been prouder of him—he was so much like his father. She put out a steadying hand.

"Let's do as the man says, Jamie. Come with me," she said gently, ushering the boy ahead of her. She looked behind her one more time at the closed and barred door she'd walked in through. Damien was on the other side of that, but that wasn't the way they were heading—they were going out an open doorway that opened up onto the mountain-side.

She walked out onto a large terrace, about the size of a large swimming pool but shaped like a half-moon—and, beyond the terrace, the void.

Shit.

It was spectacularly beautiful, and also incredibly scary. Thankfully Jamie didn't seem to understand just how close they were to the edge.

Chapter 22

Damien

Damien literally had to restrain himself from running after Tess as she disappeared into the mountain hut.

What if that madman kills her? What if he—

His phone vibrated in his pocket, interrupting his dark thoughts. He remembered he'd put it on silent.

"I'm two pitches from the top," Drake said. Damien knew, from his friend's breathless tone, just how hard he was pushing himself in the solo climb.

"Tess and Jamie are in the house with Dubois. I'm going around the hut to see if there's another way in."

"Wait for me," Drake cautioned. "Kat went back to pick up Hiro and Gael , they'll be here soon as well."

"I'll wait as long as I can," Damien told his friend, unwilling to make a promise he couldn't keep—the second Dubois called him, he was going in, no matter what.

"One officer interviewed Dubois's neighbors. Apparently Dubois's wife was sick for a long time—cancer—she died at the end of last year."

Shit.

First a dead son. Now a dead wife.

A man with nothing to lose.

"That's not good," Damien said slowly. "Does he have any remaining family members?"

"She's looking into it," Drake said, huffing.

As he disconnected the call, Damien's hand went to the lightweight Smith & Wesson J-frame revolver he'd taken from the helicopter. He made sure it was securely clipped to the back of his belt, and that the open shirt he was wearing over his black T-shirt covered it. It wasn't his preferred way to carry, but it'd have to do in this case.

His phone rang. It was Dubois's number.

"Where the hell are you? I figured you'd be storming the hut by now."

"I came alone, Dubois, as you asked."

"So you know my name," the man said. He barked out a sharp laugh. "I'll bet you don't actually remember me, or my son."

Damien forced himself to reply calmly. He couldn't afford for the situation to escalate.

"I remember your son, Roger. What happened was an unfortunate accident. Nobody was to blame. Not you and not—"

The man growled his displeasure, an animal sound that chilled Damien's blood.

"I know exactly who is to blame, and that's you, Gray. For years I watched you, hoping the universe would right things, but things just got better and better for you. You have your job, you have your son, you have a woman ... and what do I have?" His voice rose manically.

"Let's sit down and discuss this, Roger—face to face. If there's anything I did back then that you think—"

"Do not patronize me, you bastard," Dubois snarled. "I have your son and woman now. You'll do exactly as I say. Come into the house and out onto the terrace. I think you'll like the view."

Damien kicked a rock, furious at himself for not having been able to keep him on the phone for longer.

He sent a message to the team with his exact location.

Dubois wants to meet me in the terrace. I think Tess and Jamie are out there already.

Kat's reply was almost instantaneous.

Our ETA is twenty minutes.

A lot could happen in twenty minutes.

Stand by. Nobody approaches without my approval.

We've got your back, boss.

Pocketing his phone, Damien strode towards the house, half expecting to get shot at any moment—but no, Dubois had gone through too much trouble. He wanted something from Damien, and he wouldn't get that if he simply shot him now.

The door to the hut was ajar. Damien walked through, listening for any noises while he waited for his eyes to get used to the semi-darkness inside—but he could already feel the emptiness in the building.

Walking past the living space, which held a dilapidated sofa and some chairs, he arrived at what must have once been a kitchen, judging by the sink taking up one corner.

He heard a noise, coming from outside. His eyes went to the back door leading outside from the kitchen.

Jamie and Tess are out there.

Damien looked down at his phone. His team was still fifteen minutes away, probably a bit longer for Drake.

I can't wait.

Damien didn't have a game plan. In his job, that was perhaps the ultimate offence—everybody knew things could change in a second, but charging in without having a plan was simply not done.

I'm going in.

Before he could second-guess himself, Damien pushed the door open. As he stepped out into the bright sunlight, he raised a hand to shield his eyes.

When his eyes accustomed to the light, his heart froze at the sight ahead of him.

#

Tess

Tess's mouth tasted bitter. Terror—the likes of which she'd never felt before—coursed through her veins as she watched Jamie hanging over the abyss.

The boy was strapped to a rope harness, held in place only by the madman's tenuous hold on the rope. As soon as they'd walked out onto the terrace, Dubois had forced her to her knees at gunpoint and strapped Jamie into a handmade rope harness he'd clearly prepared ahead of time.

The premeditation scared Tess more than anything else—Dubois might be crazy, but he'd planned this meticulously, and he didn't intend to let them go.

Every time Dubois waved the gun in her direction, he ended up jerking Jamie's body around. Jamie's eyes were shut tight—his face pinched in fear. The boy was less than ten feet away from her, but it might as well have been ten miles.

The metal grating dug into her knees but she barely felt it, so great was her fear. "Please. Please bring him back," Tess begged. "We can talk about whatever you want. Damien will—"

Dubois turned to look at her.

"Say his name again and I'll let him go," he threatened. "We'll see how long he takes to hit the bottom."

They heard a noise from inside the house.

"Ah, here he comes. Good—my hand was getting tired."

The door opened up and Damien walked out. His expression as he took in the scene in front of him was one of pure, unadulterated terror. Tess knew what he was seeing— his son, leaning over the edge of the abyss, and she, kneeling close to the edge.

Damien's jaw was clenched. "Dubois, please, whatever you think happened, my son is not to blame."

"Shut up and drop your weapon, Gray," snarled the man. "Carefully. Or I'll open my hand."

Damien nodded and slowly reached behind him. "Please. I'm doing what you asked." He brought out a gun, holding it with two fingers, and dropped it in front of him.

"Kick it in my direction. Away from her," Dubois ordered.

Damien quickly did as he asked. For a moment, the only sound was that of the gun sliding across the metal grating covering the terrace cement floor.

Damien licked his lips. "I know you don't want to hurt innocent people, Dubois. Let them go and you and I can stay here and talk."

No!

Nobody was paying attention to her, so Tess adjusted her legs to get her foot underneath her.

If I could just reach Jamie, then —

"What the hell do you think you're doing?" Dubois snarled, shifting his weapon towards her. "Stay still or I'll shoot you in the head. I'm an excellent shot—I've shot plenty of calves."

"Why are we here, Dubois? What do you want?" Damien asked, his deep voice successfully pulling the madman's attention back onto himself.

He wasn't looking at Tess or Jamie anymore. She knew he must be in deep turmoil inside, but on the outside, he just looked focused.

Dubois stroked his unkept gray beard for a second. "Thanks to you I lost the two people I loved most in the world: my son and my wife."

"I'm sorry about your wife," Damien said. "I know she had cancer."

"Brought on by the sorrow of losing her son, you bastard," Dubois spat out. "I'm going to give you the choice I never had—I'm going to let you decide which one of the two you think should live."

Damien's entire body was taut with tension. Tess could see in the lines of his body that he was getting ready to spring for the man.

Clearly, Dubois saw it as well.

"Move a muscle and I'll let go of this rope. That will be your decision made for you," he snarled. "You have five seconds to choose—before my hand gets tired. If you choose her, I'll let go of the rope. If you choose him, I'll shoot her where she kneels."

"Daddy!" Jamie cried out. Tess could see how hard the little boy was trying to be brave.

"It's going to be okay, son," Damien said to his son in a calm voice. "Let them go, Dubois. This is between us. It's me you're angry at."

From the floor, Tess shook. She could see what Damien was trying to do—he was trying to make himself the target. Dubois was having none of it.

"Three seconds left. You're wasting time."

Damien looked at him, his blue eyes tortured. If she lived to be a hundred—which was looking particularly unlikely at the moment—she didn't think she'd ever see this much pain in someone's gaze again.

The words were out of her mouth before she could second-guess herself.

"His son! He chooses his son! Please!"

Dubois laughed then, a loud, broken sound. "Should I listen to her, Gray? Is that what you want?" The gun moved towards her.

Tess kept her eyes on Dubois, ignoring the strangled sound coming from Damien. She felt strangely calm now. If she could save Jamie's life, then this—everything—would be worth it. "It's what he wants. Tell him, Damien—tell him now. Please."

#

Damien
The words coming out of Tess's mouth were like a dagger to his heart.

His entire life, everything he'd ever trained for, and now he couldn't help the two people he cared about most in the world.

There must be something you can do.

Damien focused on the gun in the madman's hand. It was an old gun, the kind farmers keep around for when they have to put down an injured farm animal—probably not the most trustworthy weapon, but Dubois' grip was true. This wasn't the first time he was holding it.

Numb with terror, Damien watched Dubois raise his gun towards Tess.

"Maybe you should learn what it's like to live without either of them."

Dubois's words brought Damien out of his stupor. And even though he knew he'd never get there on time to save them both, Damien leaped towards Dubois. He slammed himself onto the man's shooting arm, just as the shot went off—its sound echoing loud and dry in the mountains.

Damien didn't stop to confirm whether the shot had found its mark—his entire being was focused on the rope slipping through the madman's palm.

Damien heard his son's scream as he started falling. He knew his son's life depended on him being able to grab on to the rope. From his position belly down on the ground he had little grip, but he wrapped his palms around it, feeling the burn as it slid through his hands fast. Gritting his teeth he tightened his hold on it, using his elbows to anchor himself against the metal grating beneath him.

The rope stopped moving. Damien felt his son's weight on the end. Faint with relief, he held his son.

"Daddy!"

I've got you, son. And I'm not letting go.

A second later, Damien heard a noise behind him and realized his mistake. He'd kicked Dubois to the side, but like a newbie he hadn't incapacitated the man.

Fucking idiot.

That mistake could cost his son his life.

Damien looked around for something to anchor the rope to—just as the gun slammed onto the side of his face.

Damien saw stars. He tightened his hold on the rope, knowing it was the only thing that mattered now. The second blow came, to the back of his head this time. Damien fell onto his stomach.

With his last remaining strength he twisted his wrist, wrapping the rope around it. No matter what happened, he wouldn't be letting go.

The third blow opened a cut on his forehead. Blood poured onto Damien's eye, obscuring his vision. Still, he gritted his teeth and held on.

Out of the corner of his eyes, he saw a slim shape crawling towards the rope.

Tess, she's alive.

"Die, die!" Dubois yelled, his voice hoarse with rage.

Through a curtain of blood, Damien saw the madman reach down—the sight of the knife in his hand chilled Damien's blood.

Sharp enough to cut through the rope.

As Dubois brought down the knife, Damien shifted his free hand higher up the rope. He felt the knife point dig into the back of his hand, felt the red hot pain as it struck something that could only be bone. The agony in his hand barely registered—he'd stopped the knife from cutting the rope, and each second he could hold on to that rope, hold on to his son, was worth any amount of pain.

But Dubois was strong. With a hard pull that brought tears to Damien's eyes, Dubois freed the knife. Red blood spurted from Damien's hand and he struggled to stay conscious. He raised his arm in an arc to follow the knife, but his movements were sluggish and Dubois was faster.

This time the knife came down on the rope and sawed once, twice, three times—until the ends of the rope flew apart.

"Nooooo!" Damien wailed, watching the rope holding his son slide inexorably towards the edge.

Chapter 23

Tess

"His son! He chooses his son! Please!"

As soon as the words were out of her mouth, Tess had realized how futile they were. Dubois was toying with Damien—he wasn't planning on letting either of them live. He wanted Damien to suffer as he had suffered, and that involved taking everything away from him.

Her movements jerky and uncoordinated—she'd been kneeling for so long one of her feet had gone to sleep—Tess launched herself towards Jamie. Out of the corner of her eye she saw Damien was on his move as well, hurling himself towards Dubois.

The bullet stopped her in her tracks. It slammed into her shoulder, turning her body around and sending her crashing to the floor. Her back hit the ground hard, but she barely felt it for the all-consuming heat coming from her shoulder. The burning sensation, which couldn't yet be called pain but was quickly building up to something she'd never felt before, began to take over her focus.

Her writer's mind catalogued everything that was going on—every feeling, every sensation—trying to put words to them. She couldn't help herself, it was just the way she was built.

Her left hand touched the burning area on her right shoulder and came back bloody. She looked down. Deep red blood spurted from the wound.

On TV, when people got shot, they usually contained the bleeding by holding on to the injured area with their hand. Sometimes, a few crimson drops escaped around their fingers.

The reality, she was finding out, was much more gruesome. Blood pooled around her hand, making everything slippery, to the point where it was almost impossible to put pressure on the wound.

She gasped. Panic made it hard to breathe. She wondered if the bullet had grazed her lung.

Don't be an idiot, your lungs aren't up there.

The thought made it easier to breathe. She inhaled deeply once, twice, while the burning sensation grew into something that could only be described as red-hot agony.

If it hurts this bad, that means I'm not going into shock.

Why am I not going into shock?

"Daddy!"

The single word reminded her why she couldn't afford to go into shock. She had to get to Jamie. She pushed herself off the floor with her left hand, leaving a bloody print on the metal grating beneath her, and used the momentum to get to her knees. Her head swam a bit but she ignored it, focused on the rope.

The rope was taut—her gaze followed to where Damien was holding it. He was on his knees, wrapping the rope around one wrist. As she watched, Dubois slammed the gun onto the side of his head.

Tess watched the scene play out as if stuck in one of those sticky nightmares where your body refuses to move.

You can't help Damien.

He wouldn't want you to, anyway.

Focus on Jamie.

Saying Jamie's name helped Tess take control of her panic. Jamie was what mattered here. She half-stumbled, half-dragged herself towards the rope, knowing if Damien lost the fight she would be the only thing standing between Jamie and certain death.

And then suddenly the rope was moving—fast—towards the edge. Tess threw herself on it like a cat pouncing on a mouse.

Please, God, don't let me miss.

And then the rope was sliding through her hands. Her right arm was near useless, but she tightened her palms and turned off the part of her brain that complained at the searing pain. No matter what, she couldn't let go—wouldn't let go.

"I've got you," she gasped.

But the weight of the boy on the other end of the rope was too much, and she was quickly sliding towards the edge, with nothing to stop them from falling.

"No!" she cried out. Tears filled her eyes as she looked around her for purchase—there was nothing to be found.

"Let him go, Tess," somebody said from underneath.

Tess's mouth opened in surprise. Was she losing her mind? There was nothing under them except the void. And then, peering over the edge she saw a large shape. A man was hanging off a rope in what looked like an impossible position, pulling himself up the overhang on the strength of his fingers alone. With his other hand, he clipped a carabiner around Jamie's make-shift harness.

He looked up at her—though sweat dripped from his forehead, his gray gaze was smooth and steady.

Drake.

How the hell did he get here?

"Well done, little guy. There we go. You're hanging off me now, you can let go of that rope," he said. The gruff man's tone was softer than she'd ever heard it before.

Tess saw Jamie's little fingers, which were white from gripping the rope so hard.

"Drake?" Tess asked hesitantly.

Drake nodded. "You can let go now, Tess." His gray eyes narrowed, and she knew he was looking at the blood dripping down her injured arm.

Tess forced herself to let go of the rope she was holding, watching it fall.

"Tess, where's Damien? Is he okay?" Drake asked, his voice clipped. He seemed to be pondering his next move. "I can climb up and—"

Tess looked back and saw Damien grappling with the madman towards the back of the terrace. It wasn't safe.

"It's not safe. Take Jamie away from here, please," she begged.

Drake nodded and began loosening the rope that held him, effectively lowering both him and the boy.

"Have you ever been abseiling before, buddy?" Drake asked Jamie in a soft voice. "It'll be fun, you'll see."

Tess turned around—she needed to help Damien.

Damien

Jamie was gone—he'd failed his son. For a moment Damien couldn't find it in him to move—even breathing seemed too much of a chore. He imagined the fear in the last seconds of his son's life—the pain of knowing his father, the man who should have protected him, had failed him.

So Damien, who'd always told rescues never to give up, who'd always firmly believed that while there was life there was hope, just gave up and waited for Dubois's next blow.

It never came.

The madman seemed enraptured by Damien's pain, and in no rush to end his life.

Damien's head throbbed. He could feel his heart beating thickly in his head—a sure sign of a concussion, not that he cared. His hand bled onto the ground.

A feminine cry had him raising his head.

Tess.

She was crawling awkwardly towards him, a bloody hand on her shoulder. She mouthed something, but her voice was too weak for him to hear her words, or maybe it was his hearing that was gone.

Behind him, Dubois moved and roared his displeasure.

"Why are you still alive?" he asked Tess.

Help her.

Damien knew there'd be plenty of time to wallow in self-pity later on. But he couldn't fail Tess as well.

Ignoring the fiery agony behind his eyes, Damien shifted his head to find Dubois searching the surrounding ground, looking for something.

His gun—he's looking for his gun.

Damien stumbled to his feet.

Must protect her.

Can't let him get his hands on the gun.

Standing between her and the madman, Damien aimed a solid kick at Dubois's kneecap. The big man thumped to the ground, but was up in an instant. With his good hand, Damien threw an uppercut punch that would have felled a tree—it did nothing to Dubois except make him stagger backwards. Then Dubois pushed him and Damien found himself sprawled on his ass.

He's stronger than me.

The realization was as painful as it was unexpected— Damien was used to being strong. People relied on *him* for help—but right now he was weak like a newborn.

"How does it feel, Gray? Knowing you failed your son, and that I'm going to kill your woman as well."

Damien called on all his training and stood up to face Dubois—there would be ample time for mourning Jamie, but he needed to make sure Tess didn't meet the same fate.

"Get out of here, Tess!" he shouted. He didn't know how badly she'd been hit, if she'd even be able to follow his instructions, but he put that worry out of his mind as he launched himself on Dubois—the man might be strong, but he didn't have Damien's experience in hand to hand combat. He threw a right hook, which smacked successfully onto Dubois's jaw, making him recoil.

Dubois didn't expect him to bring his injured hand to the fight, but pain meant nothing to Damien anymore.

He made a fist with his bleeding hand and punched Dubois for all he was worth, hard enough that he knew he'd cracked a couple ribs. Dubois fell forward, winded, trying to get his lungs to open up again. Damien slammed his elbows on the bigger man's back, dropping him to his knees.

And the whole time, only one sentence played on repeat in Damien's mind.

You killed my son.

Damien pressed his advantage, hitting Dubois with everything he had, until the big man dropped to his stomach. Damien grabbed the big man's head and slammed it against the floor grating in a display of violence that stunned him. But he could feel himself growing weaker with every second, and had to disable Dubois before his strength gave up on him—he couldn't let Dubois kill Tess as well.

Finally, the man was still.

Damien's injured hand spasmed. His vision was growing dimmer, narrowing into a slim tunnel of light. There was a sharp stabbing pain behind his eyes which turned into a hot flash of agony when he moved his head. Ignoring it, Damien stumbled towards the spot where he'd last seen Tess.

She was curled on the ground, her arm outstretched. Damien grabbed onto that arm with his good hand, looking for her wrist. But his hand was shaking too badly to find a pulse there, so he followed her arm to find her neck.

There was blood everywhere—most of it seemed to come from her shoulder.

Please don't be dead.

Her pulse, rapid and thready, met his fingers. Then her eyes fluttered open—clouded by pain.

"Don't move, Tess," he said, fumbling with his cell phone. He needed to get his team here, and an ambulance. Then would be the time to mourn. Damien felt hot, desperate tears

225

rolling down his face—he knew he'd never be whole again, no matter what happened.

"… fine …" she croaked urgently, her hand tugging on his sleeve.

Ignoring the pain inside his skull, Damien brought his ear closer to her mouth to hear her words.

"Jamie's fine …"

For a moment he wondered if she might be going into shock—but her green eyes were clear.

"Jamie's fine. Drake took him," she whispered.

Damien looked towards the edge. Could he dare hope that what she was saying was true?

Tess coughed, and blood spurted from her shoulder from the movement. An instant later, her body went limp.

Damien struggled to find her pulse again, his hand slipping on blood—his or hers, he couldn't be sure.

Need to get some pressure there or she's going to die on me.

Chapter 24

Tess

Tess knew where she was even before she opened her eyes. She'd had her appendix removed a couple years earlier, and the smell of hospital disinfectant wasn't something she'd ever forget.

She tried to open her eyes, but her eyelids were glued shut and sticky.

How long have I been out?

She finally got her left eye open, but the right one refused to budge. She lifted her right hand, intending to wipe at her eye—she'd barely moved an inch when her body was racked by overwhelming pain.

Tess hissed and dropped her arm again, fighting the nausea that threatened to make her empty the contents of her stomach.

Movement next to the bed had her shifting her head towards the sound. This time, both her eyelids opened, just in time to see Damien sit up straight in an armchair. He was unshaven, his eyes bleary with sleep. Bright white bandages covered the back and side of his head.

"Tess?"

"Were you sleeping?"

He nodded. "I might have dozed for a bit. How are you feeling?"

Tess looked around the small room, careful not to move her arm again.

"Where's Jamie?" she asked.

"He's okay. He's with my dad."

"Is John okay?" she asked.

Damien smiled, showing his very white teeth. He seemed relieved about something, and Tess suddenly realized he might have been worried she wouldn't remember anything. But she remembered everything that had happened, at least until she'd passed out on the terrace.

"He's fine. He's really tough. He and Jens have made a full recovery."

"What about ..." Tess's mouth went suddenly dry. "What about Dubois?"

Damien's jaw clenched tight. "He's also going to make a full recovery. I don't know whether he'll head to prison or to a psychiatric hospital."

She nodded. There wasn't much she could say. She stared at the IV stuck in her left hand.

"Tess ..." Damien began. His thumb caressed her wrist right above the spot where the IV went in. It was interesting to note that even among all that pain, she could still feel pleasure. The movement was hypnotic, and she felt her eyelids closing.

"Is it okay if I sleep a bit more?" she asked, already half in dreamland.

"Of course. I'll be right here when you wake."

When she woke up next, Damien was standing by the window, his back to her. It gave her the perfect opportunity to admire his tight ass and long legs.

He's so sexy.

It amazed her that she could even think about sex, when she was in so much pain.

Must mean I'm getting better.

She tried to move her arm, and this time lifted it a couple inches off the bed before the pain threatened to overwhelm her.

"Tess! Don't try to move your arm—they had to dig a bullet out of your shoulder."

That explains the pain.

"How long have I been here?"

"Today is the second day."

"And you've been here this whole time?" she asked, taking in his rumpled, unkept appearance. He sported a three-day beard—it was sexy, but very unlike his usual appearance. She tried unsuccessfully to remember what he'd been wearing the last time she woke.

He shrugged. "I went home for a bit to see Jamie."

"How's he feeling?"

"Surprisingly well," Damien said, a small smile tugging on his lips that softened his entire expression. "He spent an hour with Isolde Durant yesterday. She's not a child psychologist, but she knows the kind of trauma Jamie's going through, and I think she's exactly what Jamie needs."

Damien's face suddenly took on an agonized look.

"Jamie says he knew we were coming for him."

It was Tess's turn to reach out and grab his hand. "Hey …
he was right. We *did* come for him. He knows we would have
done anything to find him."

She left out the bit where they almost all died.

"How are *you* holding up, Damien?"

"Jamie's okay. You're okay. I'm … grateful," he breathed
out.

Okay. So much for exploring our feelings.

"Drake is taking Jamie rock climbing tomorrow."

"He's doing *what*? Is he insane?" Before she could stop
herself, Tess lifted her upper body from the bed, then cried
out in pain.

Damien was by her side in an instant, helping her back
onto the pillows. "Shhh … stay still, Tess, you don't want to
rip out the stitches. They're just going bouldering. Jamie is
excited about it, and I think it's good for him to do things that
help him get back control."

She pondered this for a second—it sounded surprisingly
reasonable.

"Okay … but you'll be there as well, right, Damien?" It
was then she noticed the thick bandage on his hand and the
bandages on his head. He wasn't going to be doing any
bouldering anytime soon.

"Are you okay?" she asked.

He looked down at his hand and turned it around. "I am.
Thanks to you and Drake. You both saved Jamie, and I'll
never be able to repay you."

Tess only just stopped herself from shrugging—as a good
Brit, it was one of her favorite ways of expressing herself, but
it was going to be some time before she could do it again.

"I called your family," Damien said.

"Argh. Tell me they're not on their way over."

Damien shook his head. "Do you want them here? I appeased them temporarily with the news the doctor gave me, that you're going to make a full recovery, but they'll be on the first plane over if they don't get to speak to you this morning."

"Hand me the phone," she joked. As much as she loved her family, she didn't want them to fly over. She'd end up taking care of them, and she was too tired. She needed time and—

"Uh, Tess," Damien began. His expression was a mask of uncertainty—so unlike him. He looked down until she couldn't see his eyes anymore. "We need to talk."

She felt her stomach constrict. No good news had ever followed that sentence.

Is he going to send me away?

"I love you, Tess," he said.

I love you too.

Before she could get her lips to work, he went on, his expression infinitely tender, but also sad. It took her a second to realize he was waiting for her to say something.

"If you've changed your mind, I understand. God knows I—"

Tess felt like she'd been transported onto a different universe.

"Why ..." she swallowed, but her mouth was dry as a sponge that's been out of water too long. He was by her side in a second, offering a small straw. She took a small sip of lukewarm water—nothing had ever tasted this good to her before.

She tried again, struggling to keep her tone light rather than accusatory. "Why would you think I changed my mind?"

His upper lip quivered. "I was going to choose Jamie. I was going to—"

Is that what this is about?

She wanted to laugh out loud, but knew it would hurt her shoulder too much.

"Of course you were," she said matter-of-factly. Damien was a protector through and through. She remembered his tortured expression as he'd stepped onto the terrace. It must have killed him to think he might not be able to save both of them. But if this was what was worrying him, they could work through it together.

"Of course you were, Damien. I would have done exactly the same thing."

"You would have?" He looked confused now.

I should record all these new expressions on his face.

"I would have," she confirmed. "Because Jamie will always come first … I know neither of us could live with the alternative."

Fat, heavy tears rolled down his cheeks—he wasn't even trying to wipe them off. Tess held her hand out to him and squeezed tight, lending him her strength and her support. They sat there together for the longest time, holding each other.

"Marry me, Tess," he said, so quietly she thought she might have heard him wrong.

Is he really asking me to marry him?

Right now, in the hospital, when I haven't had a shower in days?

"Not today," he clarified, smiling softly. "In the fall. When you're better."

She lay there, open-mouthed.

"I know you're young," he continued. "I know you have choices to make, but Jamie and I—"

"Stop, Damien," she began. Ignoring the burning in her shoulder, she reached up to kiss him. He supported her back easily. The moment their lips touched was pure magic—she forgot everything, the pain, the fear, and just concentrated on the feel of his lips on hers. But something tugged at the back of her mind.

He's waiting for an answer.

"Yes," she breathed into his mouth. "I'll marry you."

Chapter 25

Damien

Damien steeled himself before turning the key and pushing the front door open. It was dark inside, but he didn't reach over to turn the lights on. He took a step forward—just as the world exploded in light, sound and color.

"Happy birthday!" a chorus of voices shouted.

Colorful confetti fell on his head.

People appeared from the kitchen, from behind the sofa—he was pretty sure his home had never held this many people before.

He recognized his team, his neighbors, all his friends. And there, standing in the center of the group, were Jamie and Tess.

Damien composed what he hoped was an expression of surprise on his face.

"What is this?" he growled.

"Happy birthday, Daddy!" Jamie said, launching himself at him.

Damien caught the boy and lifted him easily, enveloping him in a bear hug. He sniffed the little boy smell in his son's hair.

Damien's surprise at the party might be feigned—he'd known for a while that Tess and Jamie were planning something—but the pleasure of holding his son in his arms was real, and not something he'd ever take for granted again.

He looked up and met Tess's green gaze—they shared an amused look.

Damien walked around the house and out onto the backyard, exchanging a couple words with every guest. The yard had been set with a series of chairs and tables. In one of them, his father chatted animatedly to his poker friends. Damien smiled. It seemed Tess and Jamie had extended invitations to half of Chamonix.

He held a beer bottle in his left hand—his right was still heavily bandaged. Apparently, dirty knives weren't the best thing to get stabbed with, and hands were delicate as hell.

The doctors had had to dig around inside his hand twice to remove dirt and prevent an infection—not a pleasant experience. They were hopeful he'd get full use of his hand back, but were waiting for his hand to heal enough to start physical therapy in order to know for sure.

Damien forced himself to relax. His hand's recovery was fully out of his control at the moment, and it was also not an injury he would ever regret. If he hadn't managed to stall Dubois those few seconds, Drake might not have gotten there in time to save his son.

Damien looked around his backyard, enjoying the warm late summer evening, grateful beyond words that they were all safe.

A body sidled up to him. He recognized Isolde Durant, though she she'd changed the dark pantsuit she normally wore to the office for a long, flowing deep blue summer dress.

"So ... she said yes," the curvy psychologist said. He looked in the direction her eyes were looking, at the glinting diamond on Tess's hand. Damien had waited two weeks, until she'd recovered physically from the shooting, before driving to Annecy with her and putting a ring on her finger.

Tess had said she didn't need a ring, but seeing it on her finger now, glinting in the evening light, Damien was glad he'd insisted.

"You still think Jamie's okay with this?"

Isolde looked at him, as if debating how much she could share with him, always mindful of doctor patient confidentiality even though Jamie wasn't formally her patient. She wasn't a child psychologist.

"You were there when we spoke about it, Damien." They'd had a talk together, the three of them, where Damien had asked Jamie how he felt about he and Tess getting married. "Jamie loves Tess. He's already planning his list of people to invite to the wedding."

Damien groaned. He didn't want a big wedding. Tess, Jamie and himself, at the courthouse, would suit him just fine. But if this surprise party was anything to go by, that wasn't the way things were going to go.

"Relax, Damien. It's going to be okay. Jamie's going to be okay."

"Is that your professional opinion?"

Isolde shook her head. "Just the opinion of a friend," she said.

Damien caught sight of Drake, standing a few feet away, an intense expression on his face.

"Drake," Damien said, calling to his friend.

Visibly shaking himself, Drake walked over. "Great party, Damien. Dr. Durant," he said, inclining his head towards the doctor.

A pinched look crossed Isolde's face, then her features were smooth again.

"Thank you for the suggestion that we take Jamie climbing, Isolde," Damien said. "He and Drake have been bouldering at Medonnet a few times, and I think he's enjoying it."

"Jamie's an amazing kid," Drake said.

Isolde's dark red lips relaxed into a smile. "I'm glad. He doesn't need to be coddled, Damien. He needs you to be there for him, and he needs to feel confident in everything he is able to do."

Damien nodded. He understood now, perhaps better than he'd ever done before, what lack of control could do to a person.

She turned to Drake, her look assessing. "Drake helped save his life. Jamie will trust him. It's good that he's involved in rebuilding the boy's confidence as well."

Damien nodded, struggling to keep his expression neutral. He still woke up at night sometimes, sweating, thinking how different things could have turned out if Drake hadn't made it to the terrace on time. He'd been back to the mountain hut a couple times since the incident. What Drake had done was an amazing physical feat—nothing short of a miracle, with the time and equipment he'd had on him.

He'd said thank you to his friend—the words as true as they were inadequate. He knew Drake didn't want nor expect his thanks, but even if Damien lived to be a hundred years old, he'd never be able to pay his friend back for what he'd done.

Out of the corner of his eye, Damien watched Jamie playing with a small group of boys and girls. His friend Xavier was there, as well as several neighborhood kids. They were running circles around a patient Bailey. Her black coat shone in the soft evening light. Damien looked around, knowing if Bailey was here Hiro couldn't be far away. There he was, one of the few people who didn't yet have a drink in their hand.

"Looks like they're trying her patience," Damien remarked to Hiro.

"Don't worry about them, she'll take good care of them. Bailey loves kids and has a soft spot for your son, anyway."

"How's your hand, boss? You coming back to work soon?" Kat asked. In her hand, she balanced a fruity-looking cocktail.

"Better. I'll be back in the office on Monday, though I'm not yet cleared for active duty."

"Where did you get that?" Hiro asked, looking at the glass in Kat's hand.

"Jens made it for me," Kat says. "He's an expert barman, didn't you know?" She turned around and called out. "Rémy! Hey, join us."

Rémy sauntered towards them—his blond, almost white hair was tied back with a scrunchie to keep it out of his face.

"Great party, Damien. Happy birthday."

"Is that water?" Kat asked in mock disgust, looking at the glass in the mountain guide's hand.

Rémy nodded sheepishly. He was well-known for being almost obsessive about what he put into his body.

The conversation flowed easily. Some instinct made Damien turn towards the sliding patio doors. There stood Tess in her jeans shorts and a sparkly short-sleeved top. Her blond hair fell in soft waves down to the middle of her back.

It was hot tonight. Damien knew the reason she wasn't wearing one of her strappy tops was that she was still self-conscious about the healing scar on her shoulder. He wanted to show her that the scar didn't matter—that it didn't mean anything—or if it did, it was simply a sign of her courage and love for him and for Jamie.

It still amazed him that this wonderful woman could have fallen in love with him and his son—Damien wanted to go down on his knees and thank his lucky stars.

And to think that he could have lost both of them just two weeks earlier … he wiped his hand angrily across his eyes— he wasn't about to start crying like a baby in front of all his friends and colleagues.

Tess sidled closer to him, as if sensing he needed her near.

"So, how do you like your surprise birthday party?" she asked, her eyes twinkling. In her hand, she held a glass of sparkling water topped with a lime wedge. Damien knew she was still taking painkillers to cope with her healing shoulder.

"I love it," he answered truthfully.

"Jamie did most of it, you know?"

Damien made a show of looking around him at the elaborate decorations that had transformed the backyard. Now that the sun had set, the space glowed by the light of dozens of strategically placed candles. Enormous platters of food graced a set of tables placed against a wall.

"You didn't help at all?" he asked, arching his eyebrow.

Tess laughed.

"Maybe a little." Her front teeth came out to bite her lower lip softly. Damien's cock jumped to attention.

Down, boy, that isn't meant for you.

He wanted nothing more than to take her to bed.

"Think they'll notice if we disappear for a bit?" The words were out before he could stop himself.

Tess's pupils grew wide.

"You haven't touched me since ..."

Her eyes filled with moisture.

"Hey, honey," Damien said, bringing her into his arms, careful not to press onto her injured shoulder. "I'm just giving you time to recover. You know how much I want you, right?"

He aligned his hips against her front so she could feel his desire.

"You really think we can—"

Suddenly they were surrounded by children. Jamie came right between them, effectively disentangling Damien from Tess.

"Dad, I need to show my friends Tess's ring."

Jamie grabbed Tess's left wrist and lifted it.

"See?"

"It's really sparkly," a little girl said. Damien recognized her vaguely as a neighbor's child.

"My dad bought it for Tess—it means she's going to become my mom."

"Wow, cool," a little boy said. "I didn't know that's how it worked."

Jamie smiled, clearly proud of himself.

"Come on, let's go get some dessert!" another child yelled.

Jamie dropped Tess's hand. As quickly as they'd arrived, the kids left, leaving Damien and Tess alone again.

"So—where were we?" Damien asked.

Tess laughed again.

"Dream on, Damien. I'm not about to be caught in bed naked by those kids."

"Tonight?" he asked.

"Sounds like a promise." she whispered. "Let's seal it with a kiss."

-- -- -- -- -- -- --

Read on for a taste of
Mont Blanc Rescue Book 2 …

Preview: Mont Blanc Rescue Book 2

Chapter 1

Drake

Drake Jacobs tightened his hold on the mountain bike's handlebars. Until now he'd been coursing gently down the forest trail, but he'd now reached the spot where the trail became more technical—and a lot more fun.

He raised his butt off the saddle, making sure his weight was distributed evenly on the pedals as he stood on the bike, holding his hips back and head up.

Standing at six-four and over two hundred and forty pounds, most of it muscle, Drake was a big man, but he wasn't worried about his bike. He'd had it upgraded to cope with what the local bike store referred to as a *heavy-duty load*.

He thundered down the slope. This was Drake's favorite part of mountain biking, that overwhelming feeling of freedom that hit as he sped down after a hard climb.

He rode hard but kept his index fingers on the break levers in case any hikers or dogs suddenly appeared—both, he knew from painful experience, could come up out of nowhere, and while he didn't mind hitting the ground, he wasn't about to risk hitting anybody else.

His front wheel hit a small rock, threatening to send him to the ground. Drake corrected—he managed to stay on the bike, but miscalculated and grazed his arm against a nearby tree, giving himself a bark tattoo.

He hissed in pain, but didn't stop.

He'd made a bet with himself that he could make the run in two hours—he was forever making stupid bets with himself—and that wouldn't happen if he stopped to admire the view.

A quiet voice inside him whispered it was his day off—if he wanted to stop and check the damage on his arm, it's not like he had anybody waiting for him back at home.

Something glinted on the ground before him—he was moving too fast to be able to tell with certainty, but he was pretty sure what it was. He braked hard and got off his bike, backtracking a few steps to where the shiny object was— indeed, it was an energy gel wrapper. He picked it up and held it in his hand for a moment. There was nothing he hated more than people who dropped litter on the trails—or anywhere in the mountains.

He spared a couple nasty thoughts for the asshole who'd dropped the gel wrapper, knowing it wasn't going to decompose for oh, say six or seven hundred years.

Would it have killed them to stick it back in their pack until they could drop it in a trash can?

Drake dug in his own pack for the small bag he always carried to keep his trash in. He allowed himself a final uncharitable thought for the idiots who thought they needed

246

an energy gel as soon as they stepped out of their front door. If they'd bothered to research the topic at all, they'd know it takes people a long while to need —

An unfamiliar hissing sound from above had Drake raising his head in alarm. The only thing above him was the Brévent cable car, and there was no reason for that sound, unless —

Drake stared, open-mouthed, as one of the cabins plunged into the air, crashing onto the ground. In an instant, it disappeared from sight, but he could hear it tearing down trees as it tumbled down the mountain.

Fuck.

It was a scene right out of one of his nightmares.

In his hand Drake still grasped the small trash bag containing the gel wrapper that might just have saved his life, by delaying his descent those extra minutes.

Drake dumped it unceremoniously into his backpack and fished for his cell phone, praying it was properly charged. He hadn't been expecting to speak with anyone today. He dialed the local emergency number, one of only three numbers he knew by heart.

"Sir, what's your emergency?" a professional-sounding female voice asked.

"Drake Jacobs here, with the PGHM," he said, speaking loudly over the sound of screeching metal. Holding the phone to his ear, he started running down the slope.

"Sir, what's your emergency?" the operator repeated stonily.

"Please look me up. Drake Jacobs," he begged, spelling out his last name. His foot hit a rock, and he almost stumbled to the ground, barely managing to right himself while keeping the phone to his ear. "I'm below the Brévent cable car. There's been an accident."

The voice changed immediately, telling him that some alarm was already ringing somewhere.

"You're *there*?"

Drake jumped over an overturned log, following the destruction the cabin had left behind it as it slammed into the trees. Up in the air, the cabin had seemed small, but the twelve-person cabin was the size of a mini bus—there was no mistaking the path it'd taken.

"I was out here with my bike. One of the cabins just crashed into the trees and went down the mountain. I'm running towards it now," he panted.

"What did you say your name was?"

"Drake Jacobs," Drake said in a clipped voice.

"Please hold. I'm patching you in with the colonel," the voice said.

"Jacobs? Is that you?"

Drake stumbled again, this time ending up on his knees on the velvet green forest floor. He put his palm to the ground to steady himself.

"Colonel Pelegrin, the Brévent cable car is down. I repeat, the cabin just crashed into the forest."

"How far away from Plan Praz are you?" the colonel asked.

Drake knew what the man was asking—the cable car connected Plan Praz and Le Brévent. At different points in the journey, the cable car could fly anywhere between thirty and two hundred feet off the ground. There was a big difference between those two figures in terms of the likelihood of finding survivors.

Drake didn't get the chance to answer. Suddenly, he saw the cabin. It was lying sideways, crumpled and barely recognizable as what it'd once been.

Cold sweat broke on his forehead.

Not again. Not this.

Drake's mind flashed back to another cable car accident, years earlier. Different time, different place, different cable car. The familiar phantom pain in his leg struck again — he'd been feeling it less and less in recent years, but it was like an old, never-forgotten friend.

Of course you're being triggered.

A cable car fell just in front of you.

He clenched his hands into fists. He couldn't let himself slip into a full-blown panic attack — not when so much depended on him.

A screamed ripped the air — a high, pained sound that brought Drake back from his stupor.

"There's at least one person inside. I have to go, Colonel. I'm sending the exact location of the crash site."

"Be careful, Jacobs," Colonel Pelegrin said, cutting the connection.

With shaking hands, Drake shared his location. He trusted the colonel to get it to the right people. He also fired off a quick message to the team, so they'd be on alert.

The scream came again. Drake approached the wreck from the top side. The cabin balanced precariously on a ledge — several large trees had stopped its fall for now, but it could just as easily go off the edge.

He, for one, didn't want to be anywhere nearby when that happened.

#

Isolde

Dr. Isolde Durant's colleagues were looking at her like she'd just sprouted a set of antennae on her forehead, rather than simply turned up at a crash site wearing a pair of jeans and sneakers.

Yes, I have days off, and sometimes I choose to wear jeans.

She shouldn't have been surprised—most of the time the *gendarmes* only saw her in the office, where she always wore one of her professional, dark pant suits and a pair of pricey, low-heeled pumps.

Isolde purposefully didn't hang out with people outside of work—it's not that she was antisocial, but rather that her job as a police psychologist required impartiality, of the kind that was impossible to show once you'd been out sharing beers and laughs with someone.

Or once you'd been to bed with someone.

She shook her head to rid herself of the troublesome memory. That was never going to happen again.

Isolde had started working with the Chamonix police force right after finishing her PhD in Police & Public Safety Psychology seven years earlier. Policing was a dangerous, high-stress career anywhere, one where mental health issues were as common, if not more common, than physical ailments. But out here in the mountains, in one of the busiest mountain rescue services in the world, Isolde knew her job offering therapy, counseling, and stress management techniques to the brave men and women who kept the mountains safe was particularly essential.

Unlike other police psychologists, who still advocated old-fashioned counseling, Isolde didn't like to get people together in groups to discuss their feelings—everything she did was designed to avoid pathologizing normal responses to trauma.

It was her dream that some of the techniques they were trying out here would, over the next years, be implemented in other progressive police departments around the world, and lead to an improvement in officers' mental and emotional health.

Isolde was rarely out on the field, however—most of the time she worked from her office, located on the top floor of the Chamonix police station. It was only once in a while that a critical accident or rescue scene was considered such high risk that she got called in on-site to offer immediate support to first responders.

A kind of psychological first aid.

So here she was, on a Sunday morning, staring at the crumpled remains of a cable car. She looked on, horrified but unable to look away.

Nobody could have survived this.

Two firefighters stood nearby, spraying something at the remains. There was no sign of any doctors or medics around.

"Did anybody survive?" she asked the uniformed officers standing next to her, dreading the answer. The young man and woman looked up at her.

"There were only two men on board, and they're both alive, if you can believe that. The cabin was held up by those trees up there for a minute, before dropping again and ending up crashing all the way down here. They were rescued just before it happened."

Isolde looked to where they were pointing. She could see the trees that must have held it in place before it went off the ledge.

My God.

"They're both alive?"

The officer nodded. "They've both been taken to the hospital with fractures, but they were both conscious and speaking to us—a miracle, if you ask me, after falling thirty feet and tumbling down the mountain. They were lucky to get out before that last fall—that's the one that pulverized the cable car."

"I'd like to speak to the first responders," she said, amazed that they'd been able to get to the men that quickly.

"He was here just a few minutes ago."

"Check behind those trees, that's where I last saw him," the young woman said.

"*He*?" Isolde asked. "There's only one first responder?"

"Yes. Apparently he was mountain biking in the area. He was lucky not to be squashed like a bug by the falling cabin. He's one of the PGHM—big guy, with brown hair and gray eyes," the uniform supplied helpfully.

Isolde's heart sank at the description.

Drake Jacobs.

She inhaled slowly.

It can't be him.

It doesn't have to be him.

That description could fit several men.

But she knew she was kidding herself.

"Thank you," Isolde said, rubbing her palms along the side of her jeans.

Isolde didn't consider herself a coward, but she suddenly found herself hoping that Drake had left the scene already. If so, she'd catch up with him the following morning, in the office. It'd be easier to speak with him on her turf, rather than out here.

A moment later, those cowardly thoughts were cut off as Drake emerged from the trees, looking even taller and broader than she remembered. Larger than life. He was wearing shorts, which surprised her, until she remembered he'd been mountain biking. There was no sign of his bike.

Drake's hand froze on his mouth as he saw her. He straightened up and dropped it slowly, his icy gray eyes defiant. She didn't need any of her degrees to tell her that he'd gone back behind those trees to throw up.

"Are you okay?" she asked. There was no need to introduce herself to him. He knew exactly who she was and why she was here. The two of them had lived through this before, albeit many years earlier.

Before she could help herself, her eyes went down to his right calf. Though it'd healed in the six years since she'd last seen the injury, it was still gruesome to look at. The scar started just below the knee and worked its way down ten inches of his leg before tapering to smooth flesh. It was a messy scar, jagged in some areas and bulging in others, the kind no surgeon would ever be proud of.

He caught her looking and scowled at her.

"What do you think? Not as neat as you expected?"

I'm amazed you can stand, let alone do what you do.

Drake took a step towards her, and Isolde suddenly felt very small. Which was interesting, because *small* was not an adjective she'd ever associated with herself. At five-six, she

253

might be average height for a woman, but she'd always been solid—of course, most people weren't six-four, either.

"I'm sorry for what happened, Drake," she said, suddenly needing to clear the air between them. If anything, his eyes got even colder—he knew she wasn't talking about anything that had happened today.

"You're sorry?" he asked tightly. "I shared things with you. And you took that information and used it to almost ruin my career."

She nodded. "I'm sorry you took it that way. I didn't see how I could give a favorable report after—"

"There's nothing I want to say to you about what happened six years ago, Dr. Durant," he said. "You're here to talk about what happened today, right? So let's do it."

The sight of his scar and the smell of whatever it was that fireman had been spraying on the vehicle played on her mind, threatening to bring her back to that other crash site, years ago.

Isolde made a fist, curling her nails into her palms, hoping the pain would steady her, but her muscles were barely responding. Something squeezed her chest—hard—as the forest started to close in on her, cold and oppressive.

Isolde knew dozens of techniques to help stop panic attacks, but suddenly couldn't bring any of them to mind.

I can't breathe.

I need to get out of here.

"We could speak tomorrow," she said, her voice tinny to her own ears.

"No time like the present, Doc," he replied, a sour smile playing on his full lips. He took a step forward, his cold gray eyes fixed on hers.

Isolde took an unconscious step backwards.

Chapter 2

Drake

Drake stared at Isolde, waiting for her to make some witty comeback—the psychologist was smart as a whip. It was one of the things he'd liked about her all those years ago—one of many things, if he was honest with himself.

He admired her legs in those tight jeans she was wearing—he had to admit, they did amazing things for her curves. It was difficult to believe, but Isolde was even more beautiful now than she'd been when they'd met, six years earlier. Still curvy and soft in all the right places, but somehow more grown up now. Her eyes were the color of pure honey, a dramatic contrast against her dark hair—some strands were tied back, as usual, to keep it out of her eyes, while the rest fell loose over her shoulders. One strand had gotten free and was falling over her eyes.

He was close enough to smell her soft, feminine perfume. Close enough that he could almost reach out and pull that rebel strand out of her eyes. Drake shook himself. He had no business looking at her like that,.

Remember what she did.

"Shall we get started? Do you want to know where the bodies were lying when I found them?"

When she didn't reply to his taunt, he stared at her more closely. She was pale, much paler than she'd been just minutes earlier, her lips bleached to an almost blue tone. Her small hands were clenched into fists—her chest heaved and her whole body shook as she struggled to take in her next breath.

All of Drake's righteous anger disappeared as he realized what he was looking at.

Jesus, she's being triggered.

And you're the asshole making it worse.

"Isolde?" he asked, hating the way his voice sounded so gruff when he spoke to her. "Isolde," he repeated firmly.

She raised her eyes towards him—the pupils dilated so the entire center of her eye looked black, with only a thin honey-colored ring at the edges. But at least she was reacting to his words.

"I think I'm going to—"

Pass out? Vomit?

Drake placed one hand gently on Isolde's back and led her to the trees he'd just walked out of, ready to pick her up if she fell. He avoided the particular tree where he'd stopped to retch a few minutes earlier, and guided her to a nearby one. As soon as they were out of sight, he placed his hands under her arm pits, gently encouraging her down into a sitting position.

She felt solid in his arms, real—he tried not to think about how close her breasts were to his hands.

"Sit down, Isolde, before you fall."

"I can't, somebody will—"

Her eyes, as she looked up at him, were panicked.

He understood her reserve.

"There's nobody here, Isolde. Just us," he said as gently as he could. "There, put your head between your knees—that's great. Now try to breathe gently."

He moved back to give her space and waited, clenching his fists, as she struggled to get air into and out of her lungs. He had half a mind to go find Jens, their team's doctor, who was somewhere around.

What the hell do you know about anxiety?

She might need more support than you're able to provide.

Isolde looked up and shook her head softly—she'd always had an uncanny ability to read his mind.

Finally, her breaths slowed down enough that Drake thought she might be able to hear to his words.

"It's not the same as last time," he said quietly.

She raised her head from between her knees. "*Quoi?*"

"I said, it's not the same as last time. The two men were alive and conscious when I got them out. One hurt his ankle, the other one hurt his shoulder. They're fine—or at least, Jens thinks they'll both make a full recovery."

"How did you—"

"I got lucky," he said, not wanting to get into the details of how he'd only just managed to drag the second man out when the cabin went off the ledge and rolled another fifty feet further down the mountain. Knowing that wouldn't make Isolde feel safer—and that's what she needed, to feel safer, more in control.

"It's not like last time," she repeated, like a mantra. "It's not like last time."

Something clenched inside Drake's chest.

So arrogant.

Why did I assume I was the only one whose life changed that day?

Author's Note

Rising 4,809 meters above sea level, Mont Blanc is the highest mountain in the Alps and second highest peak in Europe. It's one of the most majestic mountain ranges in the world—a beautiful, striking place, and one of the last wild regions in Europe.

Mont Blanc is considered by many to be the birthplace of modern mountaineering. It's easily accessible to visitors, and over 30,000 people summit every year—but it's not by any means an easy hike. Mont Blanc is a high-altitude mountain, and the danger is very real.

In real life, as in my story, the PGHM of Chamonix is the search and rescue service that responds to emergencies on Mont Blanc and on neighboring peaks. It's the world's busiest alpine-rescue team, running hundreds of rescue missions a year. These men and women are the real-life heroes that inspired my story.

Beyond that, anybody who's been to the area will know I've taken liberties with specific locations and details. I hope those liberties add to the story rather than detract from it.

Acknowledgements

So many people supported me as I wrote this book.

As always, thanks go first to my beta readers, thank you for always being there to read my work, and for your thoughtful but also gentle feedback. You made this book so much better.

To my editor—thank you for working your magic on my story. Any errors remaining are my own, as always.

To my proofreaders. This time I was sure you weren't going to find anything—once again you proved me wrong, so thank you.

Thanks to my ARC readers, for reading the book so fast, for your feedback, and for helping me understand what works best in the book.

Thanks to Maria Spada, from *Maria Spada Book Cover Design*, for the beautiful cover.

Most importantly, to you, the reader, thank you for taking a chance together with me on this new series. I hope you enjoyed meeting the Mont Blanc Rescue team, and that you'll join me as they continue their adventures.

Printed in Great Britain
by Amazon

32348385R00145